PENGUIN BOOKS

Maigret in Court

Georges Joseph Christian Simenon was born on
12 February 1903 in Liège, Belgium. He began work
as a reporter for a local newspaper at the age of sixteen, and at nineteen he moved to Paris to embark
on a career as a novelist. He started by writing pulp-
fiction novels and novellas published, under various
pseudonyms, from 1923 onwards. He went on to
write seventy-five Maigret novels and twenty-eight
Maigret short stories. Although Simenon is best
known in Britain as the writer of the Maigret books,
his prolific output of over 400 novels made him a
household name and institution in Continental
Europe, where much of his work is constantly in
print. The dark realism of Simenon's books has lent
them naturally to screen adaptation. Simenon died
in 1989 in Lausanne, Switzerland, where he had lived
for the latter part of his life.

GEORGES SIMENON

Maigret in Court

Translated by Robert Brain

PENGUIN BOOKS

PENGUIN BOOKS

Published by the Penguin Group
Penguin Books Ltd, 80 Strand, London WC2R 0RL, England
Penguin Group (USA) Inc., 375 Hudson Street, New York, New York 10014, USA
Penguin Group (Canada), 90 Eglinton Avenue East, Suite 700,
Toronto, Ontario, Canada M4P 2Y3
(a division of Pearson Penguin Canada Inc.)
Penguin Ireland, 25 St Stephen's Green, Dublin 2, Ireland
(a division of Penguin Books Ltd)
Penguin Group (Australia), 250 Camberwell Road, Camberwell, Victoria 3124,
Australia (a division of Pearson Australia Group Pty Ltd)
Penguin Books India Pvt Ltd, 11 Community Centre,
Panchsheel Park, New Delhi – 110 017, India
Penguin Group (NZ), cnr Airborne and Rosedale Roads, Albany,
Auckland 1310, New Zealand (a division of Pearson New Zealand Ltd)
Penguin Books (South Africa) (Pty) Ltd, 24 Sturdee Avenue,
Rosebank, Johannesburg 2196, South Africa

Penguin Books Ltd, Registered Offices: 80 Strand, London WC2R 0RL, England

www.penguin.com

First published as *Maigret aux Assises* 1960
This translation first published by Hamish Hamilton 1961
Reissued, under the present title, with minor revisions, in Penguin Classics 2003
Published as a Penguin Red Classic 2006
Published as a Pocket Penguin Classic 2011
5

Copyright © Georges Simenon Ltd, 1960
Translation copyright © Georges Simenon Ltd, 1965

All rights reserved

The moral right of the translator has been asserted

Set in 9.75/13.25 pt Trump Medieval
Typeset by Rowland Phototypesetting Ltd, Bury St Edmunds, Suffolk
Printed in England by Clays Ltd, St Ives plc

Except in the United States of America, this book is sold subject
to the condition that it shall not, by way of trade or otherwise, be lent,
re-sold, hired out, or otherwise circulated without the publisher's
prior consent in any form of binding or cover other than that in
which it is published and without a similar condition including this
condition being imposed on the subsequent purchaser

ISBN-13: 978-0-141-02963-4
ISBN-10: 0-141-02963-3

To Denise

Chapter One

Had he been there two hundred times? three hundred times? or even more? He had no desire to count them, nor to recall each individual case, even the most famous of them, those which had found a place in legal history, since this was the most unpleasant part of his profession.

Yet did not most of his investigations lead in the end to the Assize Court, like today, or to the police court? He would have preferred not to know about it, at least to keep out of these last rites, to which he had never altogether become habituated.

In his office at the Quai des Orfèvres, the conflict, which most often was not decided until the small hours of the morning, was still a battle of one man against another, more or less on equal terms.

Go along a few corridors, a few staircases, and it was a different setting, another world, where words no longer held the same meaning, an abstract, hieratical universe, pompous and preposterous at the same time.

With other witnesses, he had just left the courtroom with its solemn panelling, where the light from the electric globes mingled with the greyness of a rainy afternoon. The usher, whom Maigret would have sworn had always looked as old as he did now, led them to a smaller room, like a schoolmaster leading his pupils, and gestured to the benches fastened to the walls.

Most of them went and sat down obediently and, respecting

the judge's instructions, did not utter a word, even hesitated to look at their companions.

They looked straight in front of them, tense, withdrawn, saving up their secrets until that solemn moment when, quite soon now, alone in the centre of an awesome space, they would be questioned.

It was rather like being in the vestry. As a little boy, when he had gone each morning to serve Mass at the village church, Maigret used to feel a similar nervousness as he waited to follow the priest towards the altar, lit by flickering candles. He could hear footsteps of the unseen faithful going to their pews, the sacristan walking up and down.

In the same way now, he was able to follow the ritual ceremony which was being performed beyond the door. He could recognize the voice of Judge Bernerie, the most meticulous, the fussiest of magistrates, but also perhaps the most scrupulous and the most passionate seeker of the truth. Thin and in poor health, his eyes feverish, with a dry cough, he resembled a saint in a stained-glass window.

Then came the voice of Aillevard, the procurator, who sat in the public prosecutor's bench.

Finally steps approached, those of the court usher, who opened the door a crack and called:

'Detective-Inspector Segré.'

Segré, who had not sat down, glanced across at Maigret and went into the courtroom, in his overcoat, a grey hat in his hand. The eyes of the rest followed him for a moment, thinking that it would be their turn soon and anxiously wondering how they would acquit themselves.

A small patch of colourless sky was visible through some inaccessible windows, placed so high up that they were only opened or closed with the help of a cord, and the electric light sculpted the faces beneath with blank eyes.

It was warm, but it would not have been proper to take his

overcoat off. There was this ritual, to which everyone on the other side of the door paid strict attention, and it made no difference that Maigret came only from next door, along the corridors of the gloomy Law Courts: he wore an overcoat, like the rest, and carried his hat in his hand.

It was October. The chief-inspector had only returned two days ago from his holidays, to a Paris drowning in apparently interminable rain. Back in the Boulevard Richard-Lenoir, then in his office, he would have found his feelings hard to define and there was certainly as much pleasure as sadness in coming home.

In a short while, when the judge asked him his age, he would answer:

'Fifty-three.'

And that meant that, according to regulations, he would be retired in two years' time.

He had often thought about it and often looked forward to it. But this time, on his return from his holidays, retirement was no longer a vague or distant prospect; it was a logical conclusion, ineluctable, practically immediate.

Their future, during the three weeks they had spent on the Loire, had begun to materialize when the Maigrets finally bought the house where they would spend their declining days.

It happened almost against their will. As in previous years, they had stayed at an hotel in Meung-sur-Loire where they had formed their own habits and the landlord and his wife, the Fayets, treated them as members of the family.

Notices on the walls of the little town announced the sale by auction of a house on the edge of the country. They went to see it, he and Madame Maigret. It was a very old building which, with its garden surrounded by a grey wall, reminded them of a presbytery.

They had been captivated by the blue flagged passages, the kitchen with its huge beams, three steps down from ground level, which still had its pump in one corner; the drawing-room smelt like the parlour of a convent, and throughout the house the windows, with their tiny panes, mysteriously dissected the sun's rays.

At the sale the Maigrets, standing at the back of the room, had received several curious looks, and people had been surprised when the chief-inspector had raised his hand while the villagers turned round to look . . . Going . . . Going . . . Gone!

For the first time in their lives they were property-owners and, the very next day, they arranged for the plumber and the carpenter to call.

During the last few days they had even begun to tour the local antique shops. They had bought, among other things, a wooden chest with the arms of Francis I, which they had placed in the downstairs passage, near the drawing-room door, where there was a stone chimneypiece.

Maigret had not mentioned anything about it to Janvier, nor to Lucas, not to a soul, rather as if he were ashamed to be planning his future in this way, as if it were a treasonable offence in respect of the Quai des Orfèvres.

The previous day, his office had no longer looked quite the same to him, and this morning, in the witnesses' room, listening to the echoes from the courtroom, he was beginning to feel a stranger.

In two years' time he would be going fishing, and probably playing *belote* on winter afternoons with a few cronies in a corner of a café where he had already begun to go regularly.

Judge Bernerie was putting precise questions, which the inspector from the IXth *arrondissement* police station was answering with no less precision.

On the benches, around Maigret, the witnesses, men and women, had all passed through his office and some of them had spent several hours in it. Was it because they were overwhelmed by the solemn atmosphere of the place that they seemed not to recognize him?

It was not he who would question them this time, it was true. They would not be appearing, this time, before a man like themselves, but in front of an impersonal machine, and it was even uncertain whether they would understand the questions that would be put to them.

The door half-opened. It was his turn. Like his colleague from the IXth he held his hat in his hand, and without looking to left or right, he walked up to the semi-circular balustrade of the witnesses' stand.

'Your surname, Christian names, age and profession . . .'

'Maigret, Jules, fifty-three, divisional chief-inspector at Police Headquarters, Paris.'

'You are neither related to nor employed by the accused . . . ? Raise your right hand . . . Swear to tell the truth, nothing but the truth . . .'

'I swear . . .'

He saw, on his right, the figures of the jury, their faces standing out more clearly than others in the half-light, and on the right, behind the black gowns of the barristers, the accused man, sitting between two uniformed warders, his chin on his clasped hands, staring intently at him.

They had spent long hours on their own together, the two of them, in the overheated office at the Quai des Orfèvres, and they had sometimes broken off the interrogation to eat sandwiches and drink some beer, chatting like old friends.

'Listen, Meurant . . .'

Perhaps Maigret had occasionally used '*tu*' to him?

Here, an insurmountable barrier separated them and Gaston Meurant's look was as non-committal as the chief-inspector's.

Judge Bernerie and Maigret were also acquainted, not only because they had chatted together in the corridors, but because this was the thirtieth time the one had been interrogated by the other.

It had left no trace. Each played his part as if they had been strangers, officiating in a ceremony as ancient and ritualistic as the Mass.

'It was you, divisional chief-inspector, who conducted the investigations into the facts of which the court has now been apprised?'

'Yes, your honour.'

'Please turn to the members of the jury and tell them all you know.'

'On February 28 last, at about one o'clock in the afternoon, I was in my office on the Quai des Orfèvres when I received a telephone call from the station officer of the IXth *arrondissement*. He informed me that a crime had just been discovered in the Rue Manuel, not far from the Rue des Martyrs, and that he was on his way to the scene. A few minutes later I had a call from the public prosecutor's department requiring me to go along as well and to send Technical Branch and laboratory experts there.'

Maigret heard a few coughs behind him, shoes scraping on the floor. It was the first case of the law sitting and all the seats were occupied. There were probably spectators standing at the back, near the big doors guarded by uniformed policemen.

Judge Bernerie belonged to that minority of magistrates who, applying the penal code to the letter of the law, do not content themselves with hearing a résumé in the Assize Court of the examining magistrate's findings, but go over it all again in its smallest details.

'You found the public prosecutor's staff on the premises?'

'I arrived several minutes before his surrogate. I found Inspector Segré on the spot with his assistant and two detectives from the district. Nothing whatever had been touched by any of them.'

6

'Tell us what you saw.'

'The Rue Manuel is a quiet street, middle-class, with little activity in it, which runs into the bottom of the Rue des Martyrs. The house, number 27a, is situated almost half-way along the street. The concierge's lodge is not on the ground floor, but on the landing above. The inspector, who was waiting for me, took me up to the second floor where I saw two doors opening off the landing. The one on the right was ajar and on a small copper plaque was the name: Madame Faverges.'

Maigret was aware that for Judge Bernerie every point counted, and that he must omit nothing or he would be drily called to order.

'In the hall, lit by an electric lamp of frosted glass, I noticed no disorder.'

'One moment, please! Were there, on the door, any signs of its having been forced?'

'No. Experts examined it later. The lock has been removed. It has been established that no instrument, of the type generally used to force locks, was employed on it.'

'Thank you. Please proceed.'

'The flat consists of four rooms, apart from the entrance-hall. Opposite the front door is a drawing-room; the glass door into it is hung with cream curtains. It was in this room, which leads through another glass door into the dining-room, that I saw the two bodies.'

'Where were they exactly?'

'That of the woman, who I afterwards learnt was named Léontine Faverges, was lying on the carpet, her head turned towards the window. Her throat had been cut by means of some weapon which was no longer in the room, and on the carpet there was a pool of blood more than twenty inches across. As for the child's body . . .'

'You mean, do you, the young Cécile Perrin, the four-year-old girl who normally lived with Léontine Faverges?'

'Yes, your honour. The body was curled up on a Louis Quinze sofa, her face buried beneath some silk cushions. According to the local doctor, and shortly afterwards Dr Paul as well, after an attempt to strangle her, the child was smothered by those cushions . . .'

A murmur ran through the room, but the judge had only to raise his head, run his eyes along the rows of spectators, for silence to reign again.

'After the appearance of the members of the public prosecutor's department, you stayed on in the flat with your colleagues until the evening?'

'Yes, your honour.'

'Tell us what conclusions you reached.'

Maigret hesitated only a few seconds.

'From the first, I was struck by the furnishings and the interior decoration. According to her papers, Léontine Faverges had no profession. She had a small private income and looked after Cécile Perrin, whose mother, a cabaret entertainer, could not do so herself.'

The mother, Juliette Perrin, he had noticed as he entered the room, seated in the front row of the body of the court, since she was claiming damages. Her hair was dyed red and she was wearing a fur coat.

'Tell us exactly what surprised you about the flat.'

'An unusual elegance, a special style which reminded me of certain flats in the days before the laws on prostitution. The drawing-room, for example, was over-padded, over-ripe, with a profusion of rugs, cushions, and sentimental prints on the walls. The blinds were of delicate shades, as they were also in the two bedrooms, which had more mirrors than one might ordinarily expect. I gathered, in due course, that Léontine Faverges had indeed formerly kept her flat as a place of assignation. After the new laws were passed she carried on for a while. The Vice Squad had had to take notice of her and she only gave up and ceased all activity after being fined several times.'

'Were you able to discover what financial resources she had?'

'According to the concierge, women-neighbours and every-body who knew her, she had put money aside, since she had never been a spendthrift. Her maiden name was Meurant; a sister of the accused's mother, she arrived in Paris when she was eighteen and worked for a time as a saleswoman in a department store. At twenty she married a man called Faverges, a commercial traveller, who died three years later in a motor accident. The couple were then living in Asnières. For several years the young woman was to be seen frequenting the restaurants in the Rue Royale and the Vice Squad had a record of her.'

'Have you made enquiries, amongst people she knew at that time, for anyone who might have remembered her recently and decided to attack her?'

'She was a solitary person, apparently, which is rather unusual amongst her sort. She saved her money, which enabled her, later on, to set herself up in the Rue Manuel.'

'She was sixty-two years of age when she died?'

'Yes. She had grown fat, but as far as I could judge she had retained a kind of youthful appearance and a coquettish way about her. According to the witnesses I questioned she was very attached to the little girl, whom she boarded, less for the slight income it procured her, it seems, than for fear of loneliness.'

'Did she have a bank or savings-bank account?'

'No. She had no faith in loan societies, trustees, or invest-ments of any sort, and kept everything she had at home.'

'Was the money found?'

'Very little, some change, some notes of small denomination in a handbag, and some more change in a kitchen drawer.'

'Was there a hiding-place and did you discover it?'

'Apparently there was. When Léontine Faverges was ill,

which happened two or three times over the last few years, the concierge would go up to do her housework and look after the child. On a chest of drawers in the drawing-room there was a Chinese vase with a bunch of artificial flowers in it. One day the concierge wanted to dust the flowers so she took them out of the vase and found in the bottom a linen purse which she thought contained gold pieces. From its size and weight the concierge says there must have been more than a thousand. A test was carried out in my office with a linen bag and a thousand pieces. It was apparently conclusive. I questioned the staffs of various banks in the neighbourhood. At a branch of the Crédit Lyonnais they remembered a woman, whose description corresponded to that of Léontine Faverges, who they said bought bearer-bonds at various times. One of the cashiers, named Durat, officially recognized her from a photograph.'

'So it is likely that these bonds, like the gold pieces, would have been in the flat somewhere. But you did not discover anything?'

'No, your honour. We naturally searched for fingerprints on the Chinese vase, on the drawers and more or less all over the flat.'

'With no result?'

'Only the fingerprints of the two residents and, in the kitchen, those of a delivery boy whose movements have been checked. His last delivery was on the morning of the 27th. And, according to Dr Paul, who performed the autopsy on both bodies, the crime was not committed earlier than the evening of February 27 between five and eight o'clock.'

'Have you questioned all the occupants of the building?'

'Yes, your honour. They confirmed what the concierge had already told me, in other words that Léontine Faverges had no men visitors apart from her two nephews.'

'You mean the accused, Gaston Meurant, and his brother Alfred?'

'According to the concierge, Gaston Meurant came to see her fairly regularly, once or twice a month, and his last visit had occurred about three weeks before. As for his brother, Alfred Meurant, he only put in rare appearances at the Rue Manuel because he was not in favour with his aunt. By questioning her neighbour across the landing, Madame Solange Lorris, a dressmaker, I learnt that a customer of hers had come to see her for a fitting on February 27, at about half past five. This person is named Madame Ernie and lives in the Rue Saint-Georges. She states that just as she was going up the stairs, a man came out of the dead woman's flat and that when he saw her, he seemed to change his mind. Instead of going downstairs he went up towards the third floor. She was unable to see his face clearly, because the staircase is badly lighted. According to her the man was wearing a navy suit and a maroon, belted raincoat.'

'Tell us how you first got into touch with the accused.'

'While my men and I were examining the flat, on the afternoon of February 28 and were starting to question the other tenants, the evening papers came out with news of the crime and printed a certain number of details.'

'One moment. How was the crime discovered?'

'About noon that day, I mean February 28, the concierge was surprised not to have seen either Léontine Faverges, or the little girl, who usually attended a kindergarten nearby. She went and rang the doorbell. Receiving no answer she went up again a little later, still without result, and eventually she telephoned the police. But to get back to Gaston Meurant, the concierge only knew that he was a picture-framer and that he lived near Père-Lachaise. I had no need to start a search for him because the next morning . . .'

'That's March 1 . . .'

'Yes. The next morning, as I was saying, he turned up of his own accord at the IXth *arrondissement* police station saying

11

that he was the murdered woman's nephew, and the station sent him along to me . . .'

Judge Bernerie was not one of those judges who take notes, or during a hearing deal with their correspondence. Still less did he drowse off, and his eyes darted incessantly from the witness to the accused, with an occasional brief glance at the jury.

'Tell the court as exactly as possible of this first interview you had with Gaston Meurant.'

'He was wearing a grey suit and a fairly old fawn raincoat. He seemed slightly overawed at being in my office and I got the impression that it was his wife who had persuaded him to pay that visit.'

'Did she accompany him?'

'She stayed outside in the waiting-room. One of my inspectors came and informed me she was there, so I asked her to come in. Meurant told me he had read the newspapers, that Léontine Faverges was his aunt, and that, as he believed that he and his brother were the only near relations the murdered woman had, he thought he had better make himself known. I asked him how he got on with the old lady and he replied that they got on very well together. Still in answer to my queries, he added that his last visit to the Rue Manuel had been on January 23. He was unable to give me his brother's address since he no longer kept in touch with him.'

'So, on March 1 the accused categorically denied that he was at the Rue Manuel on February 27, the day of the crime.'

'Yes, your honour. Asked about his movements he told me that he had been working, in his studio in the Rue de la Roquette, until half past six that evening. I visited this studio in due course, and the shop as well. The shop has only a rather narrow window and is crammed with frames and engravings. A suction-bracket, at the back of the glass door, is used to hang a notice which reads: "If not here apply at the end of the yard."

An unlighted passage leads down, and there at the end is the workshop where Meurant constructed his picture-frames.'

'Is there a concierge?'

'No. The house has only two upper floors which you reach by a staircase leading off the yard. It is a very old building squeezed in between two blocks of tenements.'

One of the judge's assessors, whom Maigret did not know since he had recently arrived from the provinces, was staring straight ahead of him at the public with an air of not hearing a thing. The other, on the contrary, rosy-cheeked, white-haired, was nodding his head approvingly at Maigret's every sentence, some of which, God knows why, drew a smile of contentment from him. As for the jury, they stayed as still as if they had been, for example, the painted plaster figures around a Christmas crib.

Counsel for the defence, Pierre Duché, was a young man and this was his first important case. Nervous, appearing always about to jump to his feet, he bent over his file from time to time, covering it with notes.

Meurant alone, it might have been thought, showed a complete lack of interest in anything that was going on around him, or, more exactly, was watching this performance as if it were no concern of his.

He was a man of thirty-eight, relatively tall, broad-shouldered, with reddish-blond curly hair, blue eyes and the complexion that often goes with red hair.

All the witnesses described him as a gentle, mild-mannered person, not very gregarious, whose life was divided between his studio in the Rue de la Roquette and his flat in the Boulevard de Charonne, through the windows of which one could see the tombstones of the Père-Lachaise cemetery.

He was a pretty fair representative of the solitary artisan type, and the one thing surprising about him was the wife he had chosen.

Ginette Meurant was petite, with an excellent figure; she had that look about her, that way of pouting her lips, that kind of body which makes one automatically think of sex.

Ten years younger than her husband, she seemed even younger, and she had the childlike habit of fluttering her eyelashes as if she did not understand.

'How did the accused account for his movements between five o'clock and eight o'clock on February 27?'

'He told me that he had left his studio at about half past six, put out the shop lights and gone home on foot as he usually did. His wife was not in the flat. She had gone to the cinema, to the five o'clock showing, which was quite a common habit of hers. We have the box-office's evidence to this effect. It was a cinema in the Faubourg Saint-Antoine, where she regularly goes. When she got back, a little before eight o'clock, her husband had laid the table and prepared the evening meal.'

'Was this usual?'

'Apparently.'

'The concierge at the Boulevard de Charonne saw her tenant come in?'

'She doesn't remember. There are a score of flats in the building and at the end of the afternoon people are coming in and going out pretty frequently.'

'Did you mention the vase, the gold pieces and the bearer-bonds to the accused?'

'Not that day, but the next, March 2, when I summoned him to my office. I had only just then heard about that money from the concierge in the Rue Manuel.'

'Did the accused appear to know about it?'

'After some hesitation he eventually admitted that he did.'

'His aunt had taken him into her confidence?'

'Indirectly. I shall have to launch into a digression here. About five years ago, Gaston Meurant, apparently at his wife's prompting, gave up his trade to buy a café-restaurant property in the Rue du Chemin-Vert.'

'Why do you say "at his wife's prompting"?'

'Because, when Meurant first met her, eight years ago, she was a waitress in a restaurant in the Faubourg Saint-Antoine. It was through taking his meals there that Meurant got to know her. He married her and, according to her, insisted that she stop working. Meurant admits this too. Ginette Meurant's ambition was nevertheless to be the proprietress of a café-restaurant some day, and when the opportunity arose, she persuaded her husband . . .'

'Things went badly for them?'

'Yes. Within the first few months Meurant was forced to approach his aunt and borrow money from her.'

'Did she lend him any?'

'Several times. According to her nephew, there was, in the Chinese vase, beside the bag of gold pieces, also an old wallet containing bank notes. The sums she handed over to him were taken from this wallet. She used to laugh and call the vase her Chinese safe.'

'Have you traced the accused's brother, Alfred Meurnat?'

'I hadn't done so then. I simply knew from our files that he lived an irregular sort of existence and that he had twice been convicted for procuring.'

'Had witnesses stated that they had seen the accused in his studio on the afternoon of the crime, after five o'clock?'

'Not at that time.'

'Was he wearing a blue suit and a maroon raincoat, according to his statement?'

'No. His everyday suit, which is grey, and a light fawn gabardine which he generally puts on to go to work.'

'If I understand you aright, there was no precise piece of evidence enabling you to charge him?'

'That is correct.'

'Can you tell us what direction your investigations took during the days following the crime?'

'First of all, the past life of the murdered woman, Léontine Faverges, and the men she had known. We were also interested in the activities of the child's mother, Juliette Perrin, who, being aware of the contents of the Chinese vase, might have mentioned it to friends.'

'These enquiries produced nothing new?'

'No. We questioned everyone living in the street, as well, and all those who might have seen the murderer walk past.'

'Without result?'

'Without result?'

'So that, on the morning of March 6, your investigations had still got nowhere?'

'That is correct.'

'What happened on the morning of March 6?'

'I was in my office at about ten o'clock when I received a telephone call.'

'Who was it from?'

'I don't know. The caller was unwilling to give his name and I motioned to Inspector Janvier, who was standing beside me, to try and trace the call.'

'Were they successful?'

'No. The conversation was too brief. I only recognized the characteristic click of a public call-box.'

'Was it a man or a woman who spoke to you?'

'A man. I'd have sworn that he was speaking through a handkerchief to disguise his voice.'

'What did he say to you?'

'His actual words were: "If you want to trace the Rue Manuel murderer, ask Meurant to show you his blue suit. You'll find bloodstains on it." '

'What did you do?'

'I went along to the examining magistrate, who provided me with a search warrant. Accompanied by Inspector Janvier, I reached the Boulevard de Charonne at ten past eleven, and on the third floor I rang the bell of the Meurants' flat. Madame Meurant opened the door. She was in her dressing-grown, wearing slippers. She told us her husband was at his studio and I asked her if he owned a navy-blue suit.

'"Yes, indeed," she answered. "His Sunday suit."

'I asked to see it. The flat is comfortable, smart, with a gay look about it, but even at that time it was still untidy.

'"Why do you want to see this suit?"

'"Just a simple check-up . . ."

'I followed her into the bedroom, where she took a navy-blue suit from the wardrobe. Then I showed her the search warrant. The suit was packed away in a special bag I had brought, and Inspector Janvier filled in the usual receipts.

'Half an hour later the suit was in the hands of laboratory experts. During the course of the afternoon I was informed that it did in fact bear bloodstains on the right sleeve and on the lapel, but I had to wait until the next day before I knew if it was human blood. From noon, however, I arranged a discreet watch to be kept on Gaston Meurant and his wife.

'The next morning, March 7, two of my men, Inspectors Janvier and Lapointe, armed with a warrant for arrest, presented themselves at the studio in the Rue de la Roquette and proceeded to arrest Gaston Meurant.

'He seemed surprised. He said, without resisting:

'"There must be some misunderstanding."

'I was waiting for him in my office. His wife, in another office nearby, seemed more upset than he was.'

'Are you able, without the help of notes, to repeat, as closely as possible, the interview you had with the accused that day?'

'I think I can, your honour. I was sitting at my desk and I had left him standing. Inspector Janvier was standing beside him, whereas Inspector Lapointe was sitting ready to take down the interrogation in shorthand.

'I was busy signing letters and that took some time. Eventually I looked up and said, reproachfully:

' "That was not a very nice thing to do, Meurant. Why did you lie to me?"

'His ears had reddened. His lips moved.

' "Until now," I went on, "I didn't think you could have been guilty, not even suspected of it. But what can you expect now that I know you went to the Rue Manuel on February 27? What did you go there for? Why did you keep quiet about it?" '

The judge was leaning forward, so as to miss nothing of what would follow.

'What was his answer?'

'He mumbled, his head lowered:

' "I am innocent. They were already dead." '

Chapter Two

The judge must have made a discreet sign beckoning the court usher, who moved quietly round to behind the bench and leant over him, while Duché, the young counsel for the defence, pale and tense, tried to guess what was going on.

The judge uttered a few words only and everyone in the room gazed after him as he stared up at the windows, placed high in the walls, with cords hanging from them.

The radiators were scorching. An invisible fug, smelling increasingly of human bodies, rose from the hundreds of people, pressed elbow to elbow, from their damp clothes, their breathing.

The usher, moving like a sacristan, made his way towards one of the cords, tried to open a window. It wouldn't budge. He tugged three times more, and everyone waited in suspense, their eyes following his every movement; there was eventually a nervous laugh when he decided to try the next window.

This incident made people aware of the external world once more, seeing trickles of rain on the window-panes, clouds beyond, hearing all at once more distinctly the sound of motor cars and buses braking. At this very moment, as if to punctuate the pause, there even came the noise of an ambulance or police-car siren.

Maigret was waiting, worried, concentrating. He had taken advantage of the respite to glance across at Meurant, and, as their eyes met, he had thought he read a look of reproach in the blue eyes of the prisoner.

Not for the first time, at this same bar, the chief-inspector was feeling a kind of despondency. In his office at the Quai des Orfèvres he was still in touch with reality, and even when he was composing his report, he could believe that his sentences adherred to the truth.

Then months would pass, sometimes a year, if not two, before he found himself one fine day shut up in the witnesses' room with the people he had questioned ages ago, who were now no more than a memory to him. Were they really the same human beings, concierges, passers-by, tradesmen, who now sat there, staring vacantly, on the vestry-like benches?

Was it the same man, after months in prison, now in the dock?

They had suddenly been plunged into a depersonalized world where everyday phrases seemed no longer to be current, where the most commonplace actions were translated into cut-and-dried formulas. The judges' black robes, the ermine, the red gown of the advocate-general further increased this feeling of some ceremony with changeless ritual, where the individual counted for nothing.

Judge Bernerie, however, conducted the proceedings with the maximum of patience and humanity. He never pestered the witnesses to finish, never interrupted them when they seemed bogged down in useless detail.

Other magistrates, more rigorous, often made Maigret clench his fists with anger and powerlessness.

Even today he knew he was only giving a lifeless, sketchy semblance of the reality. Everything he had just said was true, but he had not been able to convey the weight of things, their density, their tiniest stirrings, the smell of them.

It seemed to him indispensable, for example, that those who were about to sit in judgement on Gaston Meurant should be made to perceive the atmosphere of the Boulevard de Charonne flat as it was when he had first found it.

His description, in two sentences, was of no earthly use. He had been struck, from the start, by the couple's living quarters, in that huge building full of homes and children, overlooking the cemetery.

Whose ideas had been imposed on the rooms, their decoration, their furnishing? In the bedroom, instead of a proper bed there was one of those three-cornered divans surrounded by shelves of the kind called 'cosy corners'. It was covered in orange satin.

Maigret tried to imagine the picture-frames, the craftsman busy all day in his studio, at the end of a courtyard, returning from work and coming home to this magazine-like setting: the lighting almost as subdued as in the Rue Manuel, the furniture too fragile, too smart, the pastel colours . . .

Nevertheless the books on the shelves certainly belonged to Meurant, nothing but volumes bought secondhand from bookshops or the embankment stalls: Tolstoy's *War and Peace*; eighteen bound volumes of the *History of the Consulate and the Empire*, in an old edition which already smelt of musty paper; *Madame Bovary*; a work devoted to wild animals, and next to it, a *History of the Religions of the World* . . .

Here was clearly a believer in self-education. In the same room were piles of sentimental newspapers, glossy magazines, cinema reviews, romantic novels, obviously constituting Ginette Meurant's fare, like the records, near the gramophone, which all bore the titles of popular songs.

How did they spend the evenings, she and he, and all day Sunday? What words did they exchange? What were their activities?

Maigret also realized he had not given an exact idea of Léontine Faverges nor of her flat where gentlemen with families and reputations used once to pay discreet visits and where, in order to prevent their meeting each other, they were whisked out of sight behind heavy curtains.

'*I am innocent. They were already dead . . .*'

In the courtroom, packed like a cinema, that sounded like a desperate lie, since the public, who were acquainted with the case only through the newspapers, and probably the jury too, looked on Gaston Meurant as a murderer who had not hesitated to put to death a little girl, first trying to strangle her and then, nervous because she would not die quickly enough, suffocating her beneath silk cushions.

It was barely eleven o'clock in the morning, but had these people here any notion now of the time, or even of their own private lives? Among the jurymen there was a birdseller from the Quai de la Mégisserie and a plumber who had a little business in which he worked himself with his two mates.

Was there also someone here who had been married to a woman like Ginette Meurant, and whose reading-matter, in the evenings, was similar to that of the accused?

'Please continue, chief-inspector.'

'I asked him to give me an exact account of his movements on the afternoon of February 27. At two o'clock, as usual, he opened his shop and hung up the card behind the door to ask people to call at the studio. He went through to there, worked on several frames. At four o'clock he turned on the lights and went back to the shop to light up the window. According to him still, he was in his studio when, shortly after six o'clock, he heard steps in the yard. Somebody tapped on the window.

'It was an old man, whom he says he had never seen before. He was looking for a flat, decorated frame, about sixteen inches by twenty-two, for an Italian gouache he had just bought. Meurant says he showed him mouldings in various sizes. After asking about the price the old man is then said to have left.'

'Has this witness been found?'

'Yes, your honour. Only three weeks afterwards. He is called

Germain Lombras, a piano teacher, who lives in the Rue Picpus.'

'Have you questioned him personally?'

'Yes, your honour. He states that he did indeed go to Meurant's studio a little after six o'clock one evening. He had happened to walk past the shop the very day after he had bought a Neapolitan landscape from an antique shop.'

'Did he tell you what the accused was wearing?'

'Apparently Meurant was wearing grey trousers under an unbleached working-smock and had taken his tie off.'

Aillevard, the procurator, in the public prosecutor's seat, who was following Maigret's testimony in a file open in front of him, was about to ask permission to speak when the chief-inspector hastened to add:

'The witness found it impossible to state exactly whether this scene took place on Tuesday or Wednesday, that's to say on February 26 or 27.'

Now it was defending counsel's turn to become agitated. The young lawyer, for whom everyone was predicting a brilliant future, was virtually staking it on this case. At all costs, he had to give the impression of a man sure both of himself and of the cause he was defending, and he was trying very hard to keep his hands still and not let them betray him.

Maigret went on, his voice impersonal:

'The accused claims that after this visit he shut up the studio, then the shop, before going off in the direction of the bus-stop.'

'Which would place his departure at about six-thirty?'

'Near enough. He got off the bus at the bottom of the Rue des Martyrs and made his way to the Rue Manuel.'

'Did he have any special reason for visiting his aunt?'

'At first he told me he hadn't, that it was just an ordinary visit, such as he was in the habit of making at least once a month. Two days later, however, when we discovered about the unhonoured bill of exchange, he went back on his statement.'

'Tell us about this bill of exchange.'

'On the 28th Meurant was due to honour a fairly substantial bill of exchange. He did not possess the necessary funds.'

'Was this bill of exchange presented?'

'Yes.'

'Was it met?'

'No.'

The advocate-general gestured as if to sweep away this argument in Meurant's favour, while Pierre Duché turned to the jury with the air of calling them to witness.

The fact had worried Maigret, too. If the accused, after cutting his aunt's throat and suffocating little Cécile Perrin, had taken away the gold pieces and the notes hidden in the Chinese vase, if he had appropriated the bearer-bonds as well, at a time when he was still not under suspicion and might well think he never would be, why had he not met the bill and avoided the risk of being declared bankrupt?

'My detectives have calculated the time it takes to get from the Rue de la Roquette to the Rue Manuel. By bus you would have to reckon about half an hour at that time of day, and by taxi you need twenty minutes. Enquiries amongst taxi-drivers have led to nothing; nor have those amongst bus conductors. Nobody remembers seeing Meurant.

'According to his subsequent statements, which he has signed, he arrived at the Rue Manuel at a few minutes before seven. He met nobody on the stairs, did not see the concierge. He knocked on his aunt's door, was surprised, after getting no answer, to see the key in the lock.

'He went in and found the scene previously described.'

'Were the lights on?'

'The main standard lamp in the drawing-room, with its salmon-pink shade, was on. Meurant thinks there were lights on in other rooms, but it is simply an impression he got, because he did not enter them.'

'How does he explain his behaviour? Why didn't he trouble to call a doctor, to warn the police . . . ?'

'For fear of being accused. He noticed a drawer in the Louis Quinze desk open and he shut it. In the same way he put back in the Chinese vase the artificial flowers which were lying on the floor. As he was about to leave he realized that through what he had done he had probably left fingerprints and he wiped the piece of furniture, then the vase, with his handkerchief. He also wiped the door-handle and, finally, before going down the stairs, he took the key away with him.'

'What did he do with it?'

'He threw it down a drain.'

'How did he get home?'

'By bus. The route for the Boulevard de Charonne runs through quieter streets, and apparently he was in his flat by twenty-five to eight.'

'His wife was not there?'

'No. As I have said she had gone to a local cinema for the five o'clock showing. She went to the cinema a lot, nearly every day. Five box-office girls remembered her on seeing her photograph. While he waited for her Meurant started reheating the remains of a joint and some runner beans, then laid the table.'

'Was that a common occurrence?'

'Quite common.'

He had the feeling, even with his back to the public, that everybody, especially amongst the women, was smiling.

'How many times have you interrogated the accused?'

'Five times, once for eleven hours. Once his statements were no longer inconsistent, I wrote out my report, which I handed to the examining magistrate, and since then I've had no opportunity of seeing him again.'

'He didn't write to you, when he was in prison?'

'Yes, he did. The letter has been entered in the file. He affirms, once again, that he is innocent and asks me to look after his wife.'

Maigret noticed Meurant make a slight movement and avoided meeting his eye.

'He didn't tell you what he meant by that, nor what he was afraid of on her account?'

'No, your honour.'

'Did you find his brother?'

'A fortnight after the crime in the Rue Manuel, on March 14, to be precise.'

'In Paris?'

'At Toulon, where, although he does not reside there permanently, he spends most of his time, with frequent trips along the Riviera, sometimes to Marseilles, sometimes to Nice and Menton. He was first examined by the Toulon police, on a rogatory commission. Then, when summoned to my office, he duly came, but not without insisting that his travelling expenses should be paid in advance. According to him, he hadn't set foot in Paris since January and he gave us the names of three witnesses with whom he played cards, at Bandol, on February 27. The witnesses have been heard. They belong to the same sort of world as Alfred Meurant; the underworld, as you might put it.'

'What was the date when you submitted your report to the examining magistrate?'

'The final report, together with the various statements signed by the accused, was delivered on March 28.'

They were reaching the tricky moment. Only three of them were aware of it, amongst those playing major roles. First the procurator, Justin Aillevard, whom Maigret had visited in the public prosecutor's office at five o'clock the day before. Then, apart from the chief-inspector himself, Judge Bernerie, who had also been informed the day before, later in the evening, by the advocate-general.

But there were others, unsuspected by the general public, who were also awaiting this moment: five detectives Maigret had chosen from among those less well known, some who belonged to that part of the Vice Squad generally known as the Society Section.

Since the opening of the trial they had been in the courtroom, scattered amongst the crowd at strategic points, watching the faces, keeping an eye on their reactions.

'Officially, therefore, chief-inspector, your investigations came to an end on March 28.'

'That is true.'

'Nevertheless, have you, since that date, concerned yourself with the actions and movements of persons closely or distantly connected with the accused?'

At once counsel for the defence rose ready to protest. He was probably about to point out that it was not in order to admit further evidence, against his client, which had not been entered in the depositions.

'Please be calm, *maître*,' the judge said to him. 'You will see in a moment that if I am using my discretionary powers to admit an unexpected development in this case, it is not with the intent to damage the prisoner's cause.'

The advocate-general, for his part, looked across at the young defence lawyer somewhat ironically, rather as if to protect him.

'I repeat my question. Did Chief-Inspector Maigret, after all, continue his investigations unofficially?'

'Yes, your honour.'

'On your own account?'

'With the consent of the director of Police Headquarters.'

'You kept the public prosecutor's office informed?'

'Not until yesterday, your honour.'

'Did the examining magistrate know that you were continuing to be concerned in the case?'

'I did mention it to him by the way.'

'You were not, however, acting on his instructions, nor on those of the attorney-general?'

'No, your honour.'

'It is essential that this should be clearly established. That is why I have referred to this, in some ways, complementary investigation as an unofficial one. What was your motive, chief-inspector, in continuing to employ your detectives on enquiries which the transfer of the case to the Grand Jury of the Assize Court no longer rendered necessary?'

The quality of the silence in the room had changed. Not the slightest cough could now be heard, not a single shoe shifted on the floor.

'I was not satisfied with the results obtained,' Maigret growled in a surly voice.

He couldn't say what he most deeply felt. The verb 'to satisfy' only partly expressed his thoughts. The facts, to his mind, did not cohere with the characters. How could he explain this in the solemn setting of the Assizes, where they expected precise sentences from him?

The judge had had just as long experience of criminal cases himself, longer even. Each evening he took back files to peruse in his flat on the Boulevard Saint-Germain, where the light in his study often remained on until two o'clock in the morning.

He had seen men and women of all sorts pass in and out of the dock and the witness box.

Yet weren't his contacts with life always theoretical? He had not been himself into the studio in the Rue de la Roquette, nor into the odd flat in the Boulevard de la Charonne. He did not know the swarming life that went on in those buildings, nor in the crowded streets, the bistros, the local dance-halls.

Prisoners were brought before him between two policemen

and all he knew about them he had found in the pages of a file.

Facts. Sentences. Words. But all around them – what of that?

His assessors were in the same position. The advocate-general as well. The very dignity of their functions isolated them from the rest of the world, in which they formed a little island apart.

Among the members of the jury, among the spectators, there were probably some who were better equipped to understand the character of a Meurant, but these people had no title in the matter or knew nothing of the complicated instrument of the law.

Was Maigret not, himself, on both sides of the fence at the same time?

'Before allowing you to continue, chief-inspector, I would like you to tell us what was the result of the analysis of the bloodstains. I am referring to those which were discovered on the blue suit belonging to the defendant.'

'It was human blood. Minute laboratory tests later showed that this blood and that of the victim possess a sufficient number of similar characteristics for it to be scientifically certain that they were from one and the same body.'

'In spite of that you proceeded with your investigation?'

'Partly because of that, your honour.'

The young lawyer, who had prepared to dispute Maigret's statement, could not believe his ears, remained restless, while the chief-inspector went steadily rumbling on.

'The witness who saw a man in a blue suit and a maroon raincoat leave Léontine Faverges' flat about five o'clock is positive about the time. The time has been checked besides by a shopkeeper in the neighbourhood on whom this person called before going to her dressmaker in the Rue Manuel. If one accepts Lombras' testimony, although he is less definite about the date of his visit to the Rue de la Roquette, the accused was still in his studio, wearing his grey trousers, at six o'clock. We have calculated the time necessary to get from that studio to the Boulevard de la Charonne, then the time needed to change and finally go to the Rue Manuel. It takes, at the lowest estimate, fifty-five minutes. The fact that the bill of exchange, which fell due the next day, was not met also struck a wrong note with me.'

'So you turned your attention to Alfred Meurant, the prisoner's brother?'

'Yes, your honour. At the same time my colleagues and I entered upon other enquiries.'

'Before allowing you to give us the result of them, I must be certain that they are strictly connected with the present case.'

'They are, your honour. For several weeks detectives from the Hotels Section showed certain photographs around a large number of Paris lodging-houses.'

'What photographs?'

'Alfred Meurant's, first. Then one of Ginette Meurant.'

It was the prisoner who leapt to his feet this time, indignant, and his counsel had to rise in turn to calm him and force him to sit down again.

'Give us your conclusions as briefly as possible.'

'Alfred Meurant, the prisoner's brother, is well known in certain districts, particularly around the Place des Ternes and the neighbourhood of the Porte Saint-Denis. We found his registration-cards at a small hotel in the Rue de l'Étoile, among others, where he has often stayed, but there is nothing to show that he has been in Paris after January 1.

'Finally, although he has been seen about with numerous women, nobody remembers having met him in his sister-in-law's company, at least during a period that goes back more than two years.'

Maigret sensed Meurant looking at him hostilely; the man had clenched both his fists, and his lawyer was continually glancing round at him for fear of an outburst.

'Please continue.'

'Ginette Meurant's photograph was recognized immediately, not only by the staffs of the cinemas, particularly the local cinemas, but also at the dance-halls both around La Chapelle and in the Rue de Lappe. She has frequented these places for many years, always in the afternoon, and the last dance-hall she has attended to date was one in the Rue des Gravilliers.'

'Used she to go to them alone?'

'She has had a certain number of boyfriends at them, never for long. However, during the last few months before the murder she was not often to be seen.'

Didn't all this evidence explain the atmosphere in the Boulevard de Charonne, the magazines and records, their contrast with the books Meurant went to buy at secondhand booksellers?

'When I left for my holidays, a little less than a month ago now,' Maigret went on, 'the various departments of Police Headquarters had discovered nothing further.'

'During this case has Madame Meurant been under surveillance by the police?'

'Not constant surveillance, in the sense that she was not followed every time she went out, and there was not always a detective outside her door at night.'

Laughter in court. A sharp look from the judge. Silence once again. Maigret wiped his brow, embarrassed by the hat he still held in his hand.

'Was this surveillance, even though sporadic,' the judge was asking, not without irony, 'the result of the letter the prisoner sent you from gaol and was it intended to protect his wife?'

'I wouldn't say that.'

'You were trying, if I understand you correctly, to discover her habits and contacts?'

'First of all I wanted to know whether she ever met her

31

brother-in-law in secret. Then, since I obtained no positive results, I wondered whom she went about with and what she did with her time.'

'One question, chief-inspector. You examined Ginette Meurant at Police Headquarters. She stated to you, if I remember correctly, that she returned home on February 27 at about eight o'clock in the evening and found dinner ready to be served. Did she tell you which suit her husband was wearing?'

'Grey trousers. He had no jacket on.'

'And when he left her after lunch?'

'He was in a grey suit.'

'At what time did she herself leave the flat in the Boulevard de Charonne?'

'About four o'clock.'

'So that Meurant might have come and changed afterwards, gone out, changed again when he returned, without her knowing?'

'It's physically possible.'

'Let's return to the subsequent investigations you had embarked upon.'

'Following Ginette Meurant revealed nothing. After her husband's imprisonment, she stayed at home most of the time, only going out to do her shopping, to visit the prison, and two or three times a week to go to the cinema. The surveillance, as I have said, was not a continuous one. It was laid on from time to time. Its results only confirm what we have been told by neighbours and tradesmen. The day before yesterday I returned from my holidays and found a report on my desk. It might be just as well to explain that the police never completely lose touch with a case, so that sometimes an arrest is made, fortuitously, two or three years after the crime or the offence.'

'In other words, during the past months, no further *systematic* investigations of the actions and movements of Ginette Meurant had been carried out?'

'That's correct. Detectives from the Hotels Section and the Vice Squad, as well as my own detectives, always carried her photograph in their pockets, however, as well as one of her brother-in-law. They would show them from time to time. It was in this manner that, on September 26, a witness recognized one of his regular clients in the photograph of the young woman.'

Meurant grew excited again and it was the judge's turn, this time, to give him a stern look. From the body of the court someone was protesting, probably Ginette Meurant.

'This witness is Nicolas Cajou, manager of a small hotel in the Rue Victor-Massé, round the corner from the Place Pigalle. He is normally in the office of his establishment and through the glass door he can keep an eye on people going in and out.'

'Wasn't he questioned last March or April, like the other hotel proprietors?'

'He was in hospital at that time, having an operation, and his sister-in-law was there in his place. Subsequently he spent three months convalescing in the Morvan, where his family come from, and it was not until the end of September that a man from the Hotels Section, just by chance, showed him the photograph.'

'Ginette Meurant's photograph?'

'Yes. He recognized her at first glance, saying that, up until he left for hospital, she used to go there with a man he did not know. One of the chambermaids, Geneviève Lavancher, also recognized the photograph.'

At the press table they turned to each other, then turned to the judge in surprise.

'I suppose the companion you alluded to is not Alfred Meurant?'

'No, your honour. Yesterday, in my office, where I asked Nicolas Cajou and the chambermaid to come, I showed them several hundred identification pictures in order to be satisfied

33

that Ginette Meurant's companion is not on our records. The man is short, thick-set, with very dark-brown hair. He dresses carefully and wears a ring with a yellow stone. He is said to be about thirty years old and he smokes American cigarettes, which he chain-smokes, so that after each of his visits to the Rue Victor-Massé the ashtray was always piled with butts, only a few of which had lipstick on them.

'I haven't had the requisite time, before the trial, to undertake a thorough investigation. Nicolas Cajou went into hospital on February 26. On the 25th he was still at the office in the hotel and he states that the couple paid a visit that day.'

There was a stir in the courtroom, unseen by Maigret, and the judge raised his voice, something he did very rarely, and pronounced:

'Silence, or I shall clear the court.'

A woman's voice tried to make itself heard:

'Your honour, I . . .'

'Silence!'

As for the prisoner, his jaw tightly set, he was looking at Maigret with hatred.

Chapter Three

Nobody stirred while the judge leaned across towards each of his assessors in turn and spoke to them in undertones. A three-way colloquy took place, which again recalled a religious rite since one could see their lips moving noiselessly as if for responses, their heads nodding in a curious rhythm. At one stage the advocate-general, in his red robe, left his seat to put in his own words, and a little later it seemed as if the young counsel for the defence was about to follow his example. He was visibly hesitating, worried, not yet quite sure of himself, and he was almost on his feet when Judge Bernerie rapped on the bench with his gavel and each magistrate resumed his position, as in a tableau.

Xavier Bernerie announced, in a low voice:

'The court thanks the witness for his testimony and asks him not to leave the courtroom.'

Still like an officiating priest, he felt around for his cap, donned it and, rising to his feet, concluded his recital:

'The hearing is adjourned for a quarter of an hour.'

The next second there was a din as of school being let out, almost an explosion, scarcely muffled at all, of sounds of all sorts jumbled together. Half the spectators left their seats; some were standing in the aisles, gesticulating; others were jostling each other in an endeavour to reach the main door which the guards had just opened, while the policemen whisked away the prisoner through an exit which was hardly distinguishable from the panelling of the walls. Pierre Duché had a struggle to follow him, and the jurors, on the other side, also disappeared behind the scene.

Barristers in gowns, most of them young, including a woman barrister who might have been a cover-girl on a magazine, formed a black and white cluster by the witnesses' entrance. They were discussing articles 310, 311, 312 and so on in the code of criminal procedure, and some of them were talking excitedly of irregularities in the conduct of the hearings, which would inevitably lead to an appeal.

An elderly barrister, with yellow teeth, in a shiny gown, an unlit cigarette hanging from his lower lip, was calmly invoking precedents, citing two cases, one at Limoges in 1885, the other at Poitiers in 1923, when not only had the preliminary investigation been entirely recast at the public trial, but when it had taken a new turning as a result of unexpected testimony.

Of all this, Maigret, a motionless block, saw only jostling figures, heard only scraps of conversation, and he hadn't had time to locate in the courtroom, where there were now several empty spaces, more than a couple of his men before he was surrounded by reporters.

The same over-excitement reigned as at the theatre, on a first night, after the first act.

'What do you think about this bombshell you've just dropped, chief-inspector?'

'What bombshell?'

He was filling his pipe methodically and he felt thirsty.

'You believe Meurant's innocent?'

'I don't believe anything.'

'You suspect his wife?'

'Gentlemen, you'll have to forgive me, but I've nothing to add to what I said in the box.'

The pack only stopped pestering him abruptly when a young reporter suddenly dashed across to Ginette Meurant who was trying to reach the exit and the rest were afraid they might miss some sensational statement.

Everybody watched the group moving along. Maigret took advantage of it to slip through the witnesses' door, came upon men smoking cigarettes in the corridor and others, unfamiliar with the building, looking for the lavatories.

He knew that the magistrates were deliberating in the Judge's Chamber; he saw an usher leading young Duché, whom they had sent for, in that direction.

It was almost noon. Bernerie obviously wanted to have the matter cleared up during the morning's hearing in order to resume the ordinary course of the trial that afternoon, hoping for a verdict the same day.

Maigret reached the gallery, lit his pipe at last, beckoned to Lapointe, whom he saw leaning against a pillar.

He was not the only one wanting to take advantage of the adjournment to have a glass of beer. Outside, people could be seen running across the street in the rain, with their collars turned up, to dive into the cafés round about.

At the Palais bar an impatient crowd, in a hurry, was disturbing those lawyers and their clients who, a few moments ago, were quietly discussing their particular business.

'Beer?' he asked Lapointe.

'If you can get any, chief.'

They thrust their way between the backs and elbows. Maigret made a sign to a waiter he had known for twenty years and a few seconds later two nicely foaming glasses of beer were passed to him over the heads of the other customers.

'See if you can find out where she has lunch, who with, who she speaks to, and who it is if she telephones to anyone.'

The tide was already ebbing and people were hurrying to get back to their seats. When the chief-inspector arrived at the courtroom, it was too late to reach the rows of benches and he had to lean against the small door, amongst the lawyers.

The jury were in their places, the prisoner as well, between his guards, his counsel lower down in front of him. The judges entered and sat down with dignity, probably conscious, like the chief-inspector, of the change that had taken place in the atmosphere.

A short time ago they had been here to deal with a man accused of having cut the throat of his aunt, a sixty-year-old woman, and having stifled, after attempting to strangle, a little four-year-old girl. Wasn't it natural that there had been a grim and somewhat stifling sense of seriousness in the air?

Now, after the interval, everything was changed. Gaston Meurant had now left the limelight and even the double crime had lost some of its importance. Maigret's evidence had introduced a new element, posed a new problem, suggestive, shocking, and the whole room now showed no interest in anything except the young woman whom the occupants of the back rows were trying in vain to glimpse.

This alone caused a buzz of noise and the judge could be seen scanning the crowd sternly, as if he were searching for the trouble-makers. This lasted a long time, but as the seconds passed the noises died down, finally disappeared altogether, silence reigned again.

'I warn the general public that I shall not tolerate any disturbance, and if there is any incident whatsoever I shall have the court cleared.'

He coughed, murmured a few words in the ears of his assessors.

'By virtue of the discretionary powers conferred upon me and in agreement with the counsels for the prosecution and the defence, I have decided to hear three new witnesses. Two are in the courtroom, and the third, the aforesaid Geneviève Lavancher, who has been summoned by telephone, will appear at this afternoon's hearing. Sergeant, will you call Madame Ginette Meurant.'

The old usher advanced, across the empty space, to meet the young woman who, sitting in the front row, rose, hesitated, then allowed herself to be led to the witness-box.

Maigret had talked to her several times at the Quai des Orfèvres. He had then had before him a young woman whose sexiness was vulgar and occasionally aggressive.

In honour of the Assize Court, she had bought herself a black tailored suit, a skirt with a three-quarter-length jacket; the only touch of colour was provided by a straw-coloured jumper.

The chief-inspector was convinced that it was also to smarten her appearance for the occasion that she was wearing a model hat which lent a kind of mystery to her face.

She seemed to be playing two roles at the same time, the naïve girl and the smart young wife, lowering her head, raising it to rest timid, docile eyes on the judge.

'Your name is Ginette Meurant, maiden name Chenault?'

'Yes, your honour.'

'Speak up and please face the jury. You are twenty-seven years old and were born at Saint-Sauveur in the Nièvre?'

'Yes, your honour.'

'You are the wife of the prisoner?'

She replied again in the same good schoolgirl voice.

'Article 322 precludes your testimony being accepted as evidence, but, with the consent of the prosecution and the defence, the court has the right to hear you for its information.'

And, as she was raising her hand in imitation of the previous witnesses, he stopped her.

'No! You do not have to take the oath.'

Between other people's heads Maigret caught a glimpse of the pale face of Gaston Meurant staring steadfastly in front of him, his chin resting in his hands. From time to time he clamped his jaws so tightly together that the bones protruded.

His wife avoided turning in his direction, as though that

were prohibited, and her eyes were fastened steadily on the judge.

'You knew the murdered woman, Léontine Faverges?'

She seemed to hesitate before murmuring:

'Not very well.'

'What do you mean by that?'

'That she and I never visited each other.'

'But you have met her?'

'The first time, before our marriage. My fiancé had insisted on introducing me to her, saying that she was all the family he had.'

'So you have been to the Rue Manuel?'

'Yes. One afternoon, about five o'clock. She gave us hot chocolate and cakes. I felt straight away that she had taken a dislike to me and that she would urge Gaston not to marry me.'

'Why was that?'

She shrugged her shoulders, searched for words, finally spoke out:

'We just weren't the same sort.'

A look from the judge halted the laughter which was about to break out.

'She did not attend your wedding?'

'Yes, she did.'

'And Alfred Meurant, your brother-in-law?'

'He, too. In those days he was living in Paris and was still on good terms with my husband.'

'What was his profession then?'

'Commercial traveller.'

'He had regular work?'

'How should I know? He gave us a coffee set as a wedding present.'

'Did you see Léontine Faverges after that?'

'Four or five times.'

'Did she come to your flat?'

'No. We used to go and see her. I never wanted to go because I hate imposing myself on people who dislike me, but Gaston maintained that I couldn't get out of it.'

'Why?'

'I don't know.'

'Was it by chance because of her money?'

'Probably.'

'When did you stop going to the Rue Manuel?'

'Ages ago.'

'Two years? Three years? Four years?'

'About three years, I suppose.'

'So you knew about the Chinese vase which was kept in the drawing-room?'

'I've seen it and I've even said to Gaston that artificial flowers ought to be kept for funeral wreaths.'

'You knew what it contained?'

'Flowers, as far as I was concerned.'

'Your husband never said anything to you?'

'What about? The vase?'

'The gold pieces.'

For the first time she turned round to the dock.

'No.'

'He did not confide in you, either, that his aunt, instead of putting her money in the bank, kept it at home?'

'I don't remember anything about that.'

'You can't be sure?'

'Oh yes ... Yes ...'

'During the period when you still paid visits to the Rue Manuel, no matter how seldom, was little Cécile Perrin already in the house?'

'I never saw her. No. She would have been too small.'

'You've heard about her from your husband?'

'He must have mentioned something about it. Wait a

minute! I'm positive now. I remember I was surprised that anybody would let a woman like her look after a baby.'

'Did you know that the prisoner fairly often went to his aunt to ask for money?'

'He didn't always tell me what he was doing.'

'But you knew about it, vaguely?'

'I knew he wasn't much of a businessman, that he could be taken in by anybody, like when we opened a restaurant in the Rue du Chemin-Vert, which might have done very nicely.'

'What did you do in the restaurant?'

'I waited on the customers.'

'And your husband?'

'He worked in the kitchen, with the help of an old woman.'

'Did he know about cooking?'

'He used a book.'

'Were you on your own in the dining-room with the customers?'

'We had a young waitress at the beginning.'

'And when things started going badly, didn't Léontine Faverges help pay off the creditors?'

'I suppose she did. I think we still owe money.'

'Did your husband seem worried towards the end of February?'

'He was always worried.'

'Did he talk to you about a bill of exchange falling due on the 28th?'

'I didn't notice. There were bills of exchange every month.'

'He didn't tell you he would be going to see his aunt to ask for help once again?'

'I don't remember it.'

'It wouldn't have struck you?'

'No. I was used to it.'

'After the restaurant was closed, you didn't suggest finding a job?'

'I did nothing else. Gaston would not allow it.'

'Why not?'

'Because he was jealous probably.'

'Did he make jealous scenes with you?'

'Not scenes.'

'Please face the jury.'

'I forgot. I'm sorry.'

'On what sort of things do you base your statement that he was a jealous man?'

'First of all, he refused to let me go out to work. Later on, in the Rue du Chemin-Vert, he kept coming up from the kitchen to spy on me.'

'Has he ever followed you?'

Pierre Duché was shifting restlessly on his bench, unable to see what the judge was driving at.

'I haven't noticed that.'

'Used he to ask you in the evenings where you'd been?'

'Yes.'

'What would you reply?'

'That I had been to the cinema.'

'Are you certain that you never talked to anybody about the Rue Manuel or Léontine Faverges?'

'Only to my husband.'

'Not to a girlfriend?'

'I have no girlfriends.'

'What people did you and your husband know?'

'Nobody.'

If these questions were flummoxing her, she gave no sign of it.

'Do you remember which suit your husband was wearing at lunch-time on February 27?'

'His grey suit. It was his everyday one. He only ever put on the other one on Saturday nights, if we went out, and on Sundays.'

'And when he visited his aunt?'

43

'Sometimes he wore his blue suit, I think.'

'He did so on that day?'

'I can't say. I wasn't in the house.'

'You don't know whether he returned to the flat during that afternoon?'

'How could I know that? I was at the cinema.'

'Thank you.'

She was still standing there, disconcerted, unable to believe that it was over, that she was not going to be asked the questions everybody was expecting.

'You may go back to your seat.'

And the judge carried on:

'Will Nicolas Cajou come forward.'

There was a feeling of disappointment in the air. The public felt that there had just been some trickery, that a scene had been cut which they had a right to watch. Ginette Meurant sat down again, almost regretfully, and a lawyer standing by Maigret was whispering to his colleagues:

'Lamblin got his claws into her in the corridor during the adjournment . . .'

Maître Lamblin, with a profile like that of a half-starved dog, was a figure who came in for quite a lot of discussion at the Palais, rarely to the good, and several times his suspension from the Bar had been mooted. As if by chance, here he was stationed beside the young woman and he was speaking to her in a low voice, as if congratulating her.

The man who was approaching the witness-box, limping, was a completely different specimen of humanity. If Ginette Meurant, underneath all her make-up, had the paleness of women who live in a hothouse atmosphere, this man was not merely pallid but his substance seemed soft and unhealthy.

Had he got so thin as a result of his operation? The fact remained that his clothes floated, much too big for him around his body which had lost all its spring and suppleness.

One could better imagine him nestling, in his slippers, in his hotel office, with its frosted windows, than walking along the city pavements.

He had bags under his eyes, loose skin under his chin.

'You are Nicolas Cajou, sixty-two years old. You were born in Marillac, in the Cantal, and you now keep a hotel in Paris, in the Rue Victor-Massé?'

'Yes, your honour.'

'You are not related to the prisoner, nor a friend of his, nor his employee . . . You swear to tell the truth, the whole truth, nothing but the truth . . . Raise your right hand . . . Say: I swear . . .'

'I swear . . .'

One of the assessors leaned towards the judge to make an observation which must have had some pertinence, for Bernerie seemed to be struck by it, pondered for a good while, finally shrugged his shoulders. Maigret, who had not missed any of this scene, guessed what was going on.

Witnesses who have been convicted with loss of civil rights, in fact, or who indulge in immoral activities, are not entitled to be sworn in. Now, was not this hotel-keeper indulging in an immoral practice, since he admitted couples to his establishment under circumstances forbidden by law? Were they sure that his police record carried no convictions?

It was too late to check up and the judge gave a small cough before asking, in an impartial voice:

'Do you normally keep a register of the visitors to whom you let rooms?'

'Yes, your honour.'

'Of *all* visitors?'

'All those who stay the night in my hotel.'

'But you do not register the names of those who only stop there during the course of the day?'

'No, your honour. The police can tell you that . . .'

That he was a law-abiding citizen, naturally, that there had never been a scandal at his place, and that occasionally he furnished the Hotels Section or Vice Squad detectives with clues they needed.

'Have you looked carefully at the witness who preceded you in the box?'

'Yes, your honour.'

'Did you recognize her?'

'Yes, your honour.'

'Tell the members of the jury of the circumstances in which you have previously seen this young woman.'

'In the usual circumstances.'

A look from Bernerie stifled the laughter.

'Which means?'

'Which means that she often appeared in the afternoon in the company of a gentleman who hired a room.'

'What do you mean by often?'

'Several times a week.'

'How many times, would you say?'

'Three or four times.'

'Her companion was always the same?'

'Yes, your honour.'

'Would you recognize him again?'

'Certainly.'

'When did you see him for the last time?'

'The day before I went into hospital, that's to say February 25. I remember the date because of my operation.'

'Describe him.'

'Not tall . . . Rather short . . . I suspect that, like others who are unfortunately short, he wore special shoes . . . Always well-dressed, a bit of a toff really . . . We know the sort round our way . . . That's just what surprised me . . .'

'What do you mean?'

'Because those gentlemen, as a rule, don't make a habit of

spending their afternoons in the hotel, specially not with the same woman . . .'

'I suppose you know all the fauna of Montmartre more or less by sight?'

'Pardon?'

'I mean the men you are talking about . . .'

'I see them go by.'

'However, you have never seen this one except in your hotel?'

'No, your honour.'

'And you haven't heard of him before?'

'I only know he's called Pierrot.'

'How do you know that?'

'Because the lady who used to come with him sometimes called him that in front of me.'

'Did he have any accent?'

'Not strictly speaking. But I always thought that he came from the south, or maybe that he was Corsican.'

'Thank you.'

This time again, disappointment was evident on people's faces. They had expected a dramatic identification and nothing happened except an apparently innocent exchange of questions and answers.

The judge looked up at the clock.

'The hearing is adjourned and will be resumed at half past two.'

The same hubbub as before, with the difference that this time the whole room was emptying and people were forming in two ranks to see Ginette Meurant pass between. It seemed to Maigret from where he was standing, at some distance, that Maître Lamblin was still following in her wake and that she kept turning around to make sure he was behind her.

The chief-inspector had hardly got outside the door when he bumped into Janvier; looked at him interrogatively.

'We've got them, chief. They're both at the Quai.'

It took the chief-inspector quite a while to realize that this referred to another case, an armed robbery at a branch of a bank in the XXth *arrondissement*.

'How did it happen?'

'Lucas arrested them at one of the boys' mother's place. The other had been hiding under the bed and the mother never knew. They hadn't been outside for three days. The poor woman thought her son was ill and kept making him hot grogs. She's the widow of a railwayman and works in a local chemist's . . .'

'How old?'

'The son, eighteen. His pal, twenty.'

'They deny it?'

'Yes. But I don't think you'll have much trouble with them.'

'What about having lunch with me?'

'I warned my wife I wouldn't be coming home, as it happened.'

It was still raining as they crossed the Place Dauphine to make their way to the brasserie which had become a kind of annex of Police Headquarters.

'How's it going at the Palais?'

'Nothing definite yet.'

They stopped at the bar, while waiting for a table to become vacant.

'I'll have to phone the judge to get his permission not to attend the trial.'

Maigret had no wish to spend the afternoon sitting motionless in the crowd, in the humid heat, listening to witnesses who, from now on, would spring no more surprises. He had heard these witnesses, all of them, in the quiet of his office. Most of them he had seen in their homes, in their proper surroundings, as well.

The Assize Court had always constituted the most un-pleasant, most depressing part of his functions, and each time he had the same feeling of misery.

Was not everything distorted there? Not through any fault of the judges, the jury, the witnesses, nor on account of the criminal code or the procedure, but because human beings were suddenly reduced, if one can so put it, to a few words, a few sentences.

He had sometimes discussed it with his friend Pardon, the local G.P. with whom he and his wife had got into the habit of dining once a month.

Once when his surgery had been full all day, Pardon had displayed a touch of discouragement, almost of bitterness.

'Twenty-eight patients in the afternoon alone! Hardly time to let them sit down, ask them a few questions. What is it you feel? Where does it hurt? How long has it been going on? The others are waiting, staring at the padded door, and wondering if their turn will ever come. Show me your tongue! Take off your clothes! In most cases an hour wouldn't be sufficient to find out everything one should know. Each patient is a separate case, and yet I have to work on the conveyor-belt system . . .'

Maigret had then told him of the end-result of his own work, in other words the Assize Court, since most investigations anyway come to their conclusion there.

'Historians,' he had remarked, 'scholars, devote their entire lives to the study of some figure of the past on whom there already exist numerous works. They go from library to library, from archives to archives, search for the least item of corres-pondence in the hope of grasping a little more of the truth . . .

'For fifty years or more they've been studying Stendhal's letters to get a clearer idea of his character . . .

'Isn't a crime almost always committed by someone out of the ordinary, in other words less easy to comprehend than the

49

man in the street? They give me a few weeks, sometimes only a few days, to steep myself in a new atmosphere, to question ten, twenty, fifty people I knew nothing at all about till then, and, if possible, to sift out the true from the false.

'I've been reproached for going myself onto the scene instead of sending my detectives. You wouldn't believe it, but it's a miracle that I'm still allowed this privilege!

'The examining magistrate, following on from me, had hardly any more scope and he only sees people, detached from their private lives, in the neutral atmosphere of his office.

'All he has in front of him, in fact, are men already reduced to mere diagrams.

'He also has only a limited time at his disposal; hounded by the press, by public opinion, his initiative restricted by a maze of regulations, submerged by administrative formalities which occupy most of his time, what is he likely to find out?

'If it is mere disincarnate beings who leave his office, what is left for the Assizes, and on what basis are the jury going to decide the fate of one or more of their own kindred?

'It's no longer a question of months or weeks, scarcely of days. The number of the witnesses is reduced to the minimum, as are the questions that are put to them.

'They come and repeat before the court a condensed version, a *digest*, as people say nowadays, of everything they have said beforehand.

'The case is merely sketched in with a few strokes, the people concerned are no more than outlines, caricatures almost . . .'

Hadn't he had that feeling once again this morning, even when he was giving his own evidence?

The press would report that he had spoken *at length* and perhaps be surprised at it. With any other judge than Xavier Bernerie, it was true, he would have been allowed only a few minutes to speak, whereas he had stayed in the witness-box for almost an hour.

He had done his best to be precise, to communicate a little of what he himself felt to those who listened to him.

He glanced through the cyclostyled menu and passed it to Janvier.

'I think I'll have the *tête de veau* . . .'

A group of detectives were standing by the bar. He noticed two lawyers in the restaurant.

'Did I tell you my wife and I have bought a house?'

'In the country?'

He had promised himself to keep quiet about this, not for the sake of making a mystery of it, but from a scruple of decency because a connection would inevitably be drawn between this purchase and his retirement which was no longer so far off.

'At Meung-sur-Loire?'

'Yes . . . It's a bit like a presbytery . . .'

In two years he would be done with the Assize Court, except perhaps on the third page of the newspapers. There he would read of the testimony of his successor, *Chief-Inspector—*

Who would, in fact, succeed him? He had no idea. They were probably starting to discuss it in higher places, but they would obviously avoid mentioning it in his presence.

'What kind of lads are these two?'

Janvier shrugged his shoulders.

'Just like the rest of them nowadays.'

Through the window-panes Maigret watched the falling rain, the grey parapet along the Seine, the motor cars sending up a bow wave of dirty water.

'How was the judge?'

'Not so bad.'

'What about her?'

'I've put Lapointe on her tracks. She's fallen into the clutches of a pretty shady lawyer, Lamblin . . .'

'Did she confess to having a lover?'

'She wasn't asked to. Bernerie is cautious.'

It was just as well to remember, in fact, that it was the trial of Gaston Meurant that was taking place at the Assizes, not that of his wife.

'Cajou recognized her?'

'Of course.'

'How did the husband take that?'

'I think he would gladly have murdered me at that moment.'

'Will he be acquitted?'

'It's too soon to tell.'

Steam rose from the plates, smoke from cigarettes, and the names of recommended wines were painted in white on the mirrors around the room.

There was one small wine from the Loire, from quite near Meung and the house like a presbytery.

Chapter Four

At two o'clock Maigret, still accompanied by Janvier, climbed the great staircase at the Quai des Orfèvres, which even in summer, on the gayest of mornings, managed to be gloomy and dim. Today a draught of damp air swept around it and the marks of wet shoes on the steps refused to dry.

Even on the first landing they could hear a faint noise from the first floor, then voices, the sound of people going to and fro could be distinguished, a sure sign that the press had been alerted and were there, with the photographers and probably television teams, perhaps cinema-newsreel men.

A case was finishing or appeared to be finishing at the Palais. A fresh one was beginning here. At one end there was already a crowd, at the other only the specialists were left.

At the Quai des Orfèvres there was also a sort of witnesses' room, the glassed-in waiting-room known as the glass cage, and the chief-inspector paused on his way past to glance in at the six people sitting there under the photographs of policemen who had died in the performance of their duty.

Was it true that all witnesses look alike? The ones here came from the same walks of life as those at the Palais de Justice, ordinary folk, modest working-class people, and two women amongst them who stared straight in front of them, their hands on their leather handbags.

The reporters charged towards Maigret, who calmed them with a movement of his hand.

'Take it easy now! Take it easy! Remember, gentlemen, that I am still in the dark about all this and I haven't even seen these lads . . .'

He pushed open his office door, promised:

'In two or three hours, maybe, if I have some news for you . . .'

He shut the door, said to Janvier:

'Go and see if Lapointe has arrived.'

He was resuming the same old habits as before his holidays, almost as much of a ritual for him as was the ceremonial of the Assizes for the magistrates. Taking off his coat and hat, he hung them in the cupboard, where there was an enamel basin where he might wash his hands. Then he sat down at his desk, fondled his pipes a little before choosing one and filling it.

Janvier returned with Lapointe.

'I'll see your two idiots in a couple of minutes.'

And to young Lapointe:

'Well, what did she get up to?'

'All the way along the corridors and down the big staircase she was surrounded by a mob of journalists and photographers, and there were others waiting for her outside. There was even a cinema-newsreel van parked by the pavement. As far as I was concerned, I could only catch a glimpse of her face once or twice through the crowd. She seemed frightened and was obviously begging them to leave her in peace.

'Suddenly Lamblin elbowed his way through the crowd, seized hold of her arm and dragged her to a taxi he had had time to go off and find. He showed her into it and the cab moved off towards the Pont Saint-Michel.

'This all happened like a conjuring trick. Unable to find a taxi myself, I couldn't follow them. However, a few minutes ago, Mace, from the *Figaro*, arrived back at the Palais. He had been lucky enough to have his car parked nearby, which meant he was able to trail the taxi.

'According to him, Maître Lamblin took Ginette Meurant

to a restaurant in the Place de l'Odéon which specializes in seafood and bouillabaisse. They lunched there on their own together, taking their time.

'And now everybody's back in their seats in the courtroom and just waiting for the Bench to arrive.'

'Go back there. Give me a ring now and then. I'd like to know whether the chambermaid's evidence provokes any incident . . .'

Maigret had been able to get in touch with the judge by telephone and had been given permission by him not to waste his time at the Palais that afternoon.

The five detectives who had been planted about the courtroom during the morning had discovered nothing. They had studied the public with the trained eye that practised judges of facial expression cast over gambling-rooms. None of the men present answered to the description furnished by Nicolas Cajou of Ginette Meurant's companion. As for Alfred Meurant, the prisoner's brother, he was not in the Palais, nor in Paris, as Maigret had now learnt from a telephone call to the Toulon flying squad.

Apart from Lapointe, who was returning to the next building by way of the internal corridors, two detectives were staying on in the courtroom, just in case.

Maigret called Lucas, who was dealing with the bank robbery.

'I thought I'd better not start questioning them until you'd had a look at them, chief. I've just arranged it so that the witnesses could catch a glimpse of them as they walked past.'

'Did they recognize both of them?'

'Yes. Particularly the one who had lost his mask, of course.'

'Bring the younger one in.'

His hair was too long, his face pimply, and he looked unhealthy and unwashed.

'Remove his handcuffs . . .'

The boy shot him a glance of defiance, obviously determined

55

not to fall into the trap which he knew was being set for him.

'Leave me alone with him now.'

In cases like this, Maigret preferred to remain alone with the suspect, and there was plenty of time, later on, for his statement to be taken down in writing and for him to be made to sign it.

He puffed away gently at his pipe.

'Sit down.'

He pushed a packet of cigarettes across to him.

'Do you smoke?'

His hand trembled. At the ends of his long, blunt fingers the nails were bitten away like a child's.

'You've lost your father?'

'It wasn't me!'

'I'm not asking whether it was you or wasn't you who organized this caper. I'm asking whether your father's alive still.'

'He's dead.'

'How did it happen?'

'In the sanatorium.'

'So your mother's keeping you?'

'I've got a job too.'

'What doing?'

'I'm a french polisher.'

It would take time. Maigret knew from experience that it was better to tackle it slowly.

'How did you get hold of the gun?'

'I've got no gun.'

'Do you want me to call in the witnesses straight away? They're waiting outside.'

'They're liars, the lot of them.'

The telephone was ringing already. It was Lapointe.

'Geneviève Lavancher has given her evidence, chief. She was asked roughly the same questions as her boss, plus one extra. The judge asked her, in fact, whether she had noticed anything special about the couple's behaviour on February 25 and she replied that she was indeed surprised to see that the bed had not been touched.'

'Are the officially listed witnesses going through yet?'

'Yes. Things are really moving fast now. They hardly get a hearing.'

It took forty minutes to break the boy's resistance; he finally burst out sobbing.

So he had been the one armed with the gun. There had been three of them, not two, for an accomplice had been waiting at the wheel of a stolen car, who had apparently planned the hold-up and had then cleared off without the others as soon as he heard the cries for help.

Nonetheless this lad, who was called Virieu, refused to give his name.

'He's older than you?'

'Yes. He's twenty-three and married.'

'He's done this sort of thing before, hasn't he?'

'That's what he said.'

'I'll have a chat with you again later, after I've heard what your chum has got to say for himself.'

Virieu was taken away. They brought in Giraucourt, his friend, who also had his handcuffs removed, and the two boys had the opportunity to exchange looks as they passed each other.

'Did he spill the beans?'

'Did you think he'd be able to keep his month shut?'

Just routine. The hold-up had misfired. No one had been killed, nobody hurt, not even any damage done, except one window-pane.

'Who had the idea of the masks?'

It hadn't been a very original idea in any case. Professional gangsters in Nice had used carnival masks when they robbed a mail van a few months ago.

'You weren't armed?'

'No.'

'Were you the one who called out when the bank-clerk came to the window: "Shoot now, you fool . . ."?'

'I don't know what I said. I lost my head . . .'

'Don't forget that your chum did what you said and pressed the trigger.'

'He didn't shoot anyone.'

'But that was only because the gun luckily failed to go off. Perhaps there wasn't a round up the spout? Perhaps the gun was faulty?'

The bank staff, together with a woman customer, had stood with their hands up. It was ten o'clock in the morning.

'It was you who called out as you went in:

' "Hands up; everyone against the wall. This is a hold-up!"

'Apparently you added:

' "This is serious." '

'I said that because a lady started to laugh.'

A woman clerk of forty-five, who was now waiting in the glass cage with the others, had seized a paperweight and thrown it out of the window, calling for help as she did so.

'Have you been convicted before?'

'Once.'

'What for?'

'For stealing a camera from a car.'

'You know what you'll cop this time?'

The young man shrugged his shoulders, trying hard to be brave.

'Five years, my lad. As for your friend, whether his gun was jammed or not, it's quite likely that he won't get away with less than ten years . . .'

This was true. The third fellow would be found some day or other. The examining magistrate would soon be on the case and since, this time, there would be no legal recess to hold up the course of justice, in three or four months' time Maigret would again be testifying before the Assize Court.

'Take him away, Lucas. There's no longer any reason to keep him separated from his friend. Let them gossip away as much as they like. Send in the first witness.'

It was only a matter of formalities now, a lot of bumph to be got through. And according to Lapointe, on the telephone, things were moving even more swiftly at the Palais, where certain of the witnesses, after only about five minutes in the box, found themselves, to their amazement, and somewhat to their disappointment, back in the crowd, trying to find a place for themselves.

At five o'clock Maigret was still working on the bank robbery, and his office, with the lights now on, was filled with smoke.

'The claim for damages is just being heard. Maître Lioran has made a short statement. In view of the unexpected developments, he is prepared to associate himself in advance with the advocate-general's closing speech.'

'And the advocate-general's speaking now?'

'He began about two minutes ago.'

'Call me back when he's finished.'

Half an hour later, Lapointe telephoned through quite a detailed account of this speech. The procurator, Aillevard, had said, in effect:

'We are here to try the prisoner, Gaston Meurant, accused of having, on February 27, cut the throat of his aunt, Léontine Faverges, then suffocated to death a four-year-old girl, Cécile Perrin, whose mother is claiming damages.'

The mother, with her henna'd hair, still wearing her fur coat, had cried out loud and had to be led, shaken with sobbing, from the courtroom.

The advocate-general had continued:

'From the witness-box we have heard some unexpected

59

evidence which we do not need to take into account as far as this case is concerned. The charges brought against the prisoner have not altered and the questions which the jury must answer still remain the same.

'Was it humanly possible for Gaston Meurant to commit this double crime and to steal the life-savings of Léontine Faverges?

'It has been established that he was aware of the Chinese vase's secret and that his aunt on several occasions took money from it to give him.

'Had he a sufficient motive?

'The day following the murder, February 28, a bill of exchange, which he had signed, fell due and he did not have the necessary funds to meet it, with the result that he was faced with bankruptcy.

'Finally, do we have proof of his presence in the flat on the Rue Manuel that afternoon?

'Six days later there was discovered, in a cupboard at his flat in the Boulevard de Charonne, a navy-blue suit belonging to him, which bore, on the sleeve and the lapel, spots of blood the origin of which he was at a loss to explain.

'According to the experts, it was human blood, and more likely than not was the blood of Léontine Faverges.

'There remains some evidence which appears to contradict this, though no aspersion is cast on the witnesses' honesty by my so putting it.

'Madame Ernie, a customer of the victim's neighbour from across the landing, saw a man dressed in a navy suit leave Léontine Faverges' flat at five o'clock that afternoon and she is almost prepared to swear that this man had very dark hair.

'On the other hand you have heard a piano teacher, Monsieur Germain Lombras, tell you that at six o'clock that evening he was with the prisoner in his studio off the Rue de la Roquette. Monsieur Germain Lombras has nevertheless admitted to us that he has a slight doubt as to the exact date of this visit.

'We have to consider a heinous crime, committed in cold blood by a man who not only attacked a defenceless woman, but did not shrink from murdering a little girl.

'There can therefore be no question of mitigating circumstances, but simply of the supreme penalty.

'It is for the jury to say, in their own hearts and minds, whether they believe Gaston Meurant to be guilty of this double crime.'

Maigret, who had at last finished with his would-be gangsters, was resigning himself to opening the door and facing the journalists.

'Have they confessed?'

He nodded his head.

'Not too much publicity, please, gentlemen. Above all don't make too much of a fuss of them! Don't let others, who might be tempted to imitate them, get the impression that these young kids have done something big. They're a wretched pair, believe me . . .'

He answered the questions, shortly, feeling heavy and tired. His mind was still half in the Assize Court, where it was the young counsel for the defence's turn to speak.

He felt tempted to push open the glass door which led through to the Palais and go and join Lapointe. But what would be the point? He could imagine the defence's final plea, which would begin like a popular novel.

Wouldn't Pierre Duché dig up as much of the past as possible?

A Le Havre family, poor, swarming with children who had to start fending for themselves as early as possible. At fifteen or sixteen the girls entered into domestic service, or rather they left home for Paris, where they were supposed to be entering into service. Had the parents the time or the means to keep an eye on them? They would write once a month, a painful scrawl with spelling mistakes, sometimes enclosing a modest postal order.

Two sisters had left home in this way, first Léontine Faverges, who had become a salesgirl in a big department store and had married soon afterwards.

Hélène, the younger, had worked in a dairy, then in a haberdasher's in the Rue d'Hauteville.

The first girl's husband had died. As for the second, she was soon finding her way about the local dance-halls.

Had they kept in touch with each other? It was doubtful. When her husband was killed in an accident, Léontine Faverges had begun to hang around the cafés in the Rue Royale and the boarding-houses round the Madeleine before setting up on her own in the Rue Manuel.

Her sister Hélène had had two children by unknown fathers and had brought them up as best she could for three years. Then she had been taken off to hospital for an operation one evening and had never left there alive.

'My client, members of the jury, educated in the Poor Schools . . .'

It was true, and Maigret could have furnished the lawyer with some interesting statistics on this subject, the percentage, for example, of pupils who went to the bad and eventually turned up in the dock in court.

These were the rebels, the ones who had a grudge against society for their humiliating circumstances.

But, contrary to what one might expect, to what the jury probably imagined, they constitute a minority.

No doubt many of the others are also affected in some way. Throughout their lives they suffer from a feeling of inferiority. But, in fact, their reaction to this is to prove to themselves that they are as good as the next man.

They have been taught a trade and they do their best to become first-class workers.

Their ambition is to have a family of their own, a proper, normal family with children to take out for a walk on Sundays.

And what sweeter revenge than to start a small firm one day, to set up on their own?

Had Pierre Duché thought about it? Was that what he was now telling them, in the courtroom where people's faces were already showing signs of fatigue?

During the long examination Maigret had been through that morning, he had left something out and now he regretted it. The conversation was, of course, all down in the file. But it was only an unimportant detail.

The third time Ginette Meurant had come to his office, at Police Headquarters, the chief-inspector had asked her incidentally:

'You have never had a child?'

She was apparently not expecting such a question, for she looked surprised.

'Why do you ask me that?'

'I don't know . . . I just have the feeling that your husband is the sort of man who would want to have children . . . Am I wrong?'

'No.'

'He did hope you would have some?'

'In the beginning, yes.'

He had sensed a hesitation, something slightly obscure, and he had delved more deeply:

'You are not able to have them?'

'No.'

'He knew this when he married you?'

'No. We had never talked about that.'

'When did he find out?'

'After a few months. Since he was always hoping and kept asking me the same question every month, I thought it better to tell him the truth . . . Not quite the whole truth . . . But the main point . . .'

'Which is?'

'That I was ill, before I met him, and had to have an operation . . .'

It had lasted like that for seven years. Though Meurant had wanted a family, they had remained simply a couple.

He had set up on his own. Later, giving in to his wife's pestering, he had tried for a while another trade than his own. As one might have expected, it had turned out disastrously. Nevertheless he had patiently built up his small picture-framing business once more.

This completed the picture for Maigret, who, rightly or wrongly, suddenly began to attach a great deal of importance to this matter of children.

He was not going so far as to maintain that Meurant was innocent. He had seen equally unobtrusive men, as quiet and gentle on the outside, become violent.

Almost always, in such cases, this was because at one time or another they had been hurt deep down, by something.

Meurant, driven by jealousy, was certainly capable of committing a *crime passionel*. It was also possible that he would have attacked a friend who had humiliated him.

Perhaps even, if his aunt had refused him money which he urgently needed . . .

Anything was possible, except, so it seemed to the chief-inspector, for a man who had so desperately wanted children, that he should slowly suffocate a little four-year-old girl.

'Hello, chief . . .'

'Yes?'

'He's finished. The Bench and the jury have retired. Some people expect they'll be out a long time. Others, though, are convinced the die is already cast.'

'How is Meurant?'

'The whole of the afternoon you might have thought it no longer concerned him. He seemed far away, his eyes clouded. When his lawyer said something to him, on two or three

64

occasions, he simply shrugged his shoulders. At the end, when the judge asked him if there was any statement he wanted to make, he didn't appear to understand. The question had to be repeated. He simply shook his head.'

'Did he look at his wife at all?'

'Not once.'

'Thank you. Now listen: did you spot Bonfils in the courtroom?'

'Yes. He's keeping close to Ginette Meurant.'

'Go and tell him to make sure he doesn't lose sight of her on the way out. In fact, to make doubly certain that he isn't given the slip, tell him to get Jussieu to help him. One of the two of them can arrange to have a car ready.'

'I understand. I'll give them your instructions.'

'She'll probably go home eventually and there must be a man permanently outside the house, in the Boulevard de Charonne.'

'And what if . . .'

'If Meurant's acquitted, Janvier, whom I'm going to send over, can look after him.'

'Do you think he . . . ?'

'I couldn't say at all, my lad.'

True enough. He had done his best. He was trying to find out the truth, but there was nothing to prove that he had found it, or even part of it.

The investigation had been conducted in March, then at the beginning of April with many hours of sunshine over Paris, light clouds, a few showers to suddenly dampen the cool mornings.

The other end of the proceedings was now taking place in an early spell of autumn weather, overcast, with rain, a low spongy sky, gleaming pavements.

To kill time, he signed some documents, went to take a look in the duty room, where he gave Janvier some instructions.

'See that you keep me informed, even in the middle of the night.'

In spite of his seeming lack of concern, he was tense, suddenly anxious, as if he were blaming himself for having undertaken too heavy a responsibility.

When the telephone rang in his office, he dashed to it.

'All over, chief!'

He could hear not only Lapointe's voice, but many different noises, quite a hubbub.

'There were four questions, two concerning each of the victims. The answer is no to all four. His lawyer, at this very moment, is trying to lead Meurant through to the clerk's office, despite the crowd which . . .'

Lapointe's voice was lost for a moment in the din.

'I'm sorry, chief . . . I grabbed the first telephone I could get at . . . I'll be along at the office as soon as possible . . .'

Maigret started walking up and down again, stuffing his pipe, changing it for another because that one didn't draw properly, opening and shutting his door again three times over.

The corridors of Police Headquarters were deserted again, and only a regular, a casual informer, sat waiting in the glass cage.

When Lapointe arrived there was still an aura of Assize Court excitement about him.

'A great many people predicted it, but it was quite a moment all the same . . . The whole room stood up . . . The little girl's mother, who had returned to her seat, fainted away and was almost trodden under foot . . .'

'Meurant?'

'He didn't seem to understand. He allowed himself to be led away without really knowing what was happening to him. The journalists who were able to get close enough didn't get a word out of him. So they descended on his wife again, with Lamblin playing her bodyguard.

'Immediately after the verdict, she tried to rush across to Meurant, as if to throw her arms around him . . . He had already turned his back on the courtroom . . .'

'Where is she?'

'Lamblin led her off to some office or other, near the barristers' robing-room . . . Jussieu's taking charge of her . . .'

It was half past six. Police Headquarters was beginning to empty, lights were being switched out.

'I'm off home to dinner.'

'What am I supposed to do now?'

'You go home to dinner too, and get some sleep.'

'Do you think anything will happen?'

The chief-inspector, who was opening his cupboard to get out his overcoat and hat, simply shrugged his shoulders.

'Do you remember the house search?'

'Clearly.'

'You're sure there were no firearms in the flat?'

'Positive. I'm convinced that Meurant has never possessed a gun in his life. He didn't even do military service, because of his eyesight . . .'

'See you tomorrow, my lad.'

'Okay, chief.'

Maigret caught a bus, then walked along past the façades of the houses in the Boulevard Richard-Lenoir, his back bent, his collar raised. When he reached the landing on his floor, the door opened, forming a rectangle of warm light and letting smells of cooking drift out.

'Happy?' Madame Maigret asked him.

'Why?'

'Because he's been acquitted.'

'How did you know?'

'I just heard it on the wireless.'

'What else did they say?'

'That his wife was waiting for him at the exit and that they took a taxi and went home.'

He ensconced himself in his familiar world, got back into his habits, his slippers.

'Are you very hungry?'

'I don't know. What's for dinner?'

He was thinking of another flat, where another couple lived, in the Boulevard de Charonne. There could be no dinner prepared over there, but probably some ham and cheese in the larder.

In the street two detectives would be walking up and down in the rain, unless they had found shelter in some doorway.

What would be happening? After living seven months in prison, what would Gaston Meurant have said to his wife? How would he be looking at her? Had he tried to kiss her, place his hands on hers?

Would she swear to him that everything they had said about her was untrue?

Or would she ask his forgiveness, swearing that she loved no one but him?

Would he go back to his shop the next day, to his picture-framing studio at the end of the courtyard?

Maigret was eating mechanically and Madame Maigret knew this was no time to ask him questions.

The telephone rang.

'Hello, yes . . . It's me . . . Vacher? . . . Is Jussieu with you? . . .'

'I'm phoning from a bar nearby to give you my report . . . I've nothing special to tell you, but I guessed you'd like to know . . .'

'Have they gone home?'

'Yes.'

'Alone?'

'Yes. A few minutes later, the lights were switched on on the third floor. I saw shadows passing to and fro behind the curtain . . .'

'And then?'

'About half an hour later his wife came down, carrying an umbrella. Jussieu followed her. She didn't go far. She went to a delicatessen, next a baker's, then she went back upstairs . . .'

'Did Jussieu see her close to?'

'Quite close, through the delicatessen window.'

'How does she seem?'

'She looked as though she'd been crying. Her cheeks were flushed, her eyes shining . . .'

'She didn't seem upset?'

'Not according to Jussieu.'

'And since then?'

'I suppose they had something to eat. I saw Ginette Meurant's silhouette again, in the room which seems to be the bedroom . . .'

'Is that the lot?'

'Yes. Shall we both stay here?'

'I think it would be wisest. I should like one of you to go upstairs and keep watch inside the building in a little while. The tenants probably go to bed early. Perhaps Jussieu could install himself on the landing, as soon as people have stopped coming in and out. He can tell the concierge, but ask her to keep quiet about it.'

'Right, chief.'

'Ring me back here in two hours, no matter what happens.'

'So long as the bar is still open.'

'If not I may call around there myself.'

There was no gun in the flat, certainly, but hadn't Léontine Faverges' murderer used a knife, which, moreover, had not been recovered? An extremely sharp knife, the experts maintained, and they thought it was probably a butcher's knife.

All the Paris cutlers, all the hardware shops had been questioned, and of course it had proved useless.

Come to think of it, they knew nothing, except that a woman and a little girl were dead, that a certain navy-blue suit belonging to Gaston Meurant had spots of blood on it, and that the man's wife, at the time of the crime, was meeting a lover several times a week in a boarding-house in the Rue Victor-Massé.

That was all. For lack of proof, the jury had just acquitted the frame-maker.

They had found it impossible to declare him guilty, but they had found it equally impossible to declare him innocent.

While her husband had been in prison, Ginette Meurant had led an exemplary life, hardly ever leaving home, never meeting anyone suspicious.

There was no telephone in their flat. Her mail had been watched, with no result.

'Are you serious about going over there tonight?'

'Just to have a little walk before going to bed.'

'Are you afraid something will happen?'

What answer could he give? That both of them were so ill-suited, living together in the strange flat where the *History of the Consulate and the Empire* stood on the shelves of the cosy-corner next to the silk dolls and the film stars' confessions.

Chapter Five

At about eleven-thirty, Maigret had stopped for a moment in a taxi in the Boulevard de Charonne. Jussieu, wearing the blank expression of men on night duty, had appeared silently out of the shadows, had pointed above them to a lighted window on the third floor. It was one of few lights still on in the neighbourhood, a district where people leave for work early in the morning.

Rain was still falling, but the drops were well spaced and there were the beginnings of a silver glow between the clouds.

'That window up there is the dining-room,' the detective had explained, smelling strongly of cigarette smoke. 'The light's been off in the bedroom for the past half-hour.'

Maigret waited a few minutes, hoping to catch a glimpse of life behind the curtain. As nothing stirred, he went home to bed.

From reports and telephone calls next day, he was to reconstruct, then follow hour by hour, every movement of the Meurants.

At six o'clock in the morning, when the concierge was bringing in the dustbins, two other detectives went to take over, although this time one did not go inside the house, for it was no longer possible to stay on the stairs during the daytime.

Vacher, who had spent the night there, sometimes sitting on a step, sometimes, if there was a sound of movement in the flat, leaning against the door, made a report that was a little disturbing.

Quite early, after a meal during which the couple had hardly exchanged a word, Ginette Meurant had gone into the bedroom to get undressed; Jussieu, who had seen her, from out in the street, pulling her dress off over her head, as if in a Chinese lantern show, confirmed this.

Her husband had not followed her. She had gone to him to say something, but then apparently went to bed while he remained sitting in an armchair in the dining-room.

Later on, several times he got up, walked around the room, stopping and starting repeatedly, only to sit down again.

Towards midnight his wife had come in and spoken to him again. From the landing Vacher could not make out what they were saying, but he recognized their voices. From the tone they were not quarrelling. It was a kind of monologue from the young woman, with an occasional very brief sentence, or just a single word, from her husband.

She had gone back to bed, still by herself, seemingly. The light still burned in the dining-room and at about half past two Ginette had returned to the charge once more.

Meurant was not asleep, since he had replied at once, laconically. Vacher thought she had wept. He had certainly heard a monotonous complaining, punctuated by characteristic sniffling.

Still without any sign of anger, the husband sent her back to bed and probably dozed off at last in the armchair.

Later, a baby had woken up on the floor above; there had been muffled footsteps, then from about five o'clock the occupants of the house had started to get up, turn on the lights; the smell of coffee had spread on to the staircase. At half past five one man was already leaving for work and looked inquisitively at the detective, who had no means of hiding, then looked at the door and seemed to understand.

It was Dupeu and Baron who took over, outside, at six

o'clock. The rain had stopped. The trees were dripping. The fog reduced visibility to about twenty yards.

The light in the dining-room was still on, the one in the bedroom off. It was not long before Meurant left the house, unshaven, his clothes crumpled, like those of a man who has spent the night fully clothed, and he had set off to the tobacconist's bar on the corner where he had drunk three cups of black coffee and eaten some croissants. Just as he was turning the door-handle to leave, he had changed his mind and, going back to the zinc counter, had ordered a cognac which he had swallowed in one gulp.

The investigations, in the spring, revealed that he was not much of a drinker, that he hardly took anything except a little wine with his meals and an occasional glass of beer in the summer.

He went by foot to the Rue de la Roquette, did not turn round to see if he was being followed. When he arrived at his shop he stopped outside a moment in front of the closed shutters, did not go in, but turned into the yard, and unlocked the door of his glass-fronted studio.

He remained standing inside for quite a time, doing nothing, just staring about him at the work-bench, the tools hooked on the wall, the hanging frames, the boards and the shavings. Water had seeped in under the door and formed a little puddle on the cement floor.

Meurant had opened the stove door, put in some kindling wood, some nuts of coal that were still left, then as he was about to strike a match he had changed his mind, gone outside again and locked the door behind him.

He had walked quite a long way, with no apparent destination. At the Place de la République he had gone into another bar where he had drunk a second brandy while the waiter kept staring at him, seemingly wondering where he had seen that face before.

Did he realize it? Two or three passers-by had also turned round to look at him, since his photograph was appearing in the papers that very morning under the headline:

GASTON MEURANT ACQUITTED

He might have seen the headline, the photograph, on all the newspaper-stands, but he did not have the curiosity to buy himself a paper. He took a bus, got out twenty minutes later at the Place Pigalle, and walked in the direction of the Rue Victor-Massé.

Finally he stopped in front of the small hotel kept by Nicolas Cajou, the Hôtel du Lion, and stood there a long time, staring at the façade.

When he began his tour again, it was to go back down towards the Grands Boulevards, walking in a vague way, sometimes stopping at crossroads as if he were not sure where to go, buying a packet of cigarettes en route . . .

Going along the Rue Montmartre, he had reached Les Halles and the detective almost lost track of him in the throng. At the Châtelet he had drunk a third cognac, in one gulp as before, and he had finally arrived at the Quai des Orfèvres.

Now that the sun had risen, the yellowy fog was becoming less thick. Maigret, in his office, received a telephone report from Dupeu, who had remained on guard at the Boulevard de Charonne.

'The wife got up at ten to eight. I saw her open the curtains, then the window, and gaze out into the street. She looked as though she was searching for her husband. She probably didn't hear him go out and was surprised to find the dining-room empty. I think she noticed me, chief . . .'

'Never mind. But if she goes out as well, make sure she doesn't give you the slip.'

On the quayside, Gaston Meurant was hesitating, looking at the windows of Police Headquarters in the same way as he had looked at those of the hotel a short while before. It was half past nine. He walked on as far as the Pont Saint-Michel, was about to cross the bridge when he retraced his steps and, going past the policeman on duty, at last came into the entrance-hall.

He was familiar with the place. He was seen to climb the grey staircase slowly, stopping, not for breath, but because he was still uncertain.

'He's on his way up, chief!' Baron telephoned, from an office on the ground floor.

And Maigret repeated to Janvier, who was with him in his office:

'He's on his way up.'

They both waited. It took a long time. Meurant could not make up his mind, wandered along the corridor, stopped outside the chief-inspector's door, as if he were about to knock on it without having himself announced.

'What are you looking for?' Joseph, the old porter, asked him.

'I'd like to speak to Inspector Maigret.'

'Come along then. You'll have to fill in a form.'

Pencil in hand, he was pondering again whether to give up and go, just when Janvier came out of Maigret's office.

'Have you come to see the chief-inspector? Follow me.'

The whole thing must have been like a nightmare for Meurant. He had the face of someone who had hardly slept, his eyes red-rimmed, and he smelt of stale smoke and alcohol. Yet he was by no means drunk. He followed Janvier. The latter opened the door for him, ushered him in ahead, and then closed it again, without going in himself.

Maigret, at his desk, apparently deep in the perusal of a file, waited for a while without raising his head, then he turned towards his visitor, without any sign of surprise, murmured:

'One moment . . .'

He wrote some notes on a document, then another, murmured distractedly:

'Sit down.'

Meurant did not sit down, did not even come forward into the centre of the room. At the end of his patience, he announced:

'I suppose you think I've come to thank you?'

His voice was not entirely natural. He was a little hoarse and he tried to put some sarcasm into his reproach.

'Sit down,' Maigret repeated, without looking at him.

This time Meurant came forward three steps, grasped the back of a chair with its seat upholstered in green velvet.

'Did you do that to save me?'

The chief-inspector finally surveyed him, calmly, from top to toe.

'You look tired, Meurant.'

'I'm not concerned with myself, but with what you did yesterday.'

His voice was more hollow, as though it was an effort for him to control his temper.

'I've come here to tell you that I don't believe a word of what you said, that you lied, like those others lied, that I'd sooner be in prison, that it was a dirty trick you played . . .'

Was it the alcohol which made him somewhat disjointed? Possibly. Yet, once again, he was not drunk, and these sentences must have been running around in his head for a good part of the night.

'Sit down.'

At last! He complied, against his will, as if he smelt a trap.

'You may smoke if you wish.'

As a protest, so as not to be obliged to the chief-inspector for anything, he did not do so, much though he wanted to, and his hand was trembling.

'It's easy for you to make people like that say what you want them to; they depend on the police . . .'

He obviously meant Nicolas Cajou, letting rooms by the hour in his hotel, and the chambermaid.

Maigret lit his pipe slowly, waited.

'You know as well as I do that it's untrue . . .'

His anguish brought out drops of sweat on his forehead. Maigret spoke at last.

'You mean to tell me that you murdered your aunt and little Cécile Perrin?'

'You know very well I didn't.'

'I don't *know* it, but I am almost convinced that you didn't. Why, do you suppose?'

Surprised, Meurant could not think of an answer.

'There are a lot of children in the building where you live in the Boulevard de Charonne, aren't there?'

Meurant said yes, mechanically.

'You hear them coming in and going out. Sometimes when they come back from school they play on the stairs. Do you talk to them sometimes?'

'I know them all right.'

'You know the school hours, although you've no children yourself. That made quite an impression on me, from the beginning of the investigations. Cécile Perrin used to attend kindergarten. Léontine Faverges went to collect her every day, except on Thursdays, at four o'clock in the afternoon. Until four o'clock therefore, your aunt was alone in the flat.'

Meurant was doing his best to follow.

'You had a large bill falling due on February 28, we know. It is possible that the last time you borrowed money from her Léontine Faverges let you know that she would not fork out again. Supposing you planned to kill her, to get your hands on the money in the Chinese vase and the bonds . . .'

'I did not kill her.'

'Let me finish. Just suppose, I'm saying, that you had conceived this idea, there would have been absolutely no point in your going to the Rue Manuel after four o'clock and consequently being obliged to kill two people instead of one.

Criminals who murder children unnecessarily are very rare and they fall into a well-defined category.'

It seemed as though Meurant, his eyes misting over, was on the point of bursting into tears.

'The murderer of Léontine Faverges and the child either was not aware of the existence of the latter or was forced to do the deed in the late afternoon. Well, if he knew of the secret of the vase and the drawer with the bearer-bonds in it, it is more than likely that he also knew of Cécile Perrin's presence in the flat.'

'What are you getting at?'

'Please have a cigarette.'

Automatically the man obeyed, but continued to look at Maigret with suspicion in his eyes, even if the anger was now dimmed.

'We're still just supposing, aren't we? The murderer knows that you're due to arrive at the Rue Manuel at about six o'clock. He is not unaware of the fact that police doctors – the newspapers have said so often enough – are capable of pin-pointing the time of death in most cases to within an hour or two.'

'Nobody knew that . . .'

His voice had altered too and he was now looking away from the chief-inspector's face.

'If he committed the crime at about five o'clock the murderer was pretty well sure that you would be suspected. He could not foresee that a customer would turn up at your studio at six o'clock and, anyhow, the music teacher was not able to supply any absolute evidence, since he isn't positive about the date.'

'Nobody knew . . .' repeated Meurant mechanically.

Maigret changed the subject suddenly.

'Do you know your neighbours at the Boulevard de Charonne?'

'I say good morning to them on the stairs.'

'They never call on you, even for a cup of coffee? You don't visit their flats? You are not on more or less friendly terms with any of them?'

'No.'

'So the chances are that they have never heard your aunt mentioned.'

'They have now!'

'But not before. Did you and your wife have many friends in Paris?'

Meurant replied with bad grace, as if he were afraid that if he conceded one point he would have to give in all along the line.

'What difference does that make?'

'Did you sometimes dine out with friends?'

'No.'

'Who did you go out with on Sundays?'

'With my wife.'

'And she has no relations in Paris. Nor have you, apart from your brother, who lives mostly in the south, and with whom you broke off all contact two years ago.'

'There was no quarrel.'

'Nevertheless you stopped seeing him.'

And once again Maigret seemed to change the subject.

'How many keys are there to your flat?'

'Two. My wife has one, I have the other.'

'It never happens that either of you leaves the key with the concierge or a neighbour when you go out?'

Meurant preferred to keep quiet, realizing that Maigret never said anything without a reason, but unable to see what he was driving at now.

'On that day the lock had not been forced, so the experts say who examined it. Yet, if you did not commit the murder, somebody entered your flat twice, the first time to get your blue suit from the wardrobe in the bedroom, and the second time to put it back, neatly enough for you to notice nothing amiss. Do you admit this?'

'I admit nothing. All I know is that my wife . . .'

'When you first met her, seven years ago, you were a lonely man. Or am I mistaken?'

'I worked all day, and in the evening I used to read, sometimes went to the cinema.'

'Did she fling herself at you?'

'No.'

'Didn't other men, other customers at the restaurant where she was a waitress, make advances to her?'

He clenched his fists.

'So what?'

'How long did it take you before she finally agreed to go out with you?'

'Three weeks.'

'What did you do, that first evening?'

'We went to the cinema, then she wanted to go dancing.'

'Are you a good dancer?'

'No.'

'Did she tease you about it?'

He didn't answer, more and more disconcerted by the turn the interview had taken.

'Afterwards you took her back to your place?'

'No.'

'Why not?'

'Because I was in love with her.'

'And the second time?'

'We went to the cinema again.'

'Afterwards?'

'To a hotel.'

'Why not to your flat?'

'Because I was living in a badly furnished room at the end of a yard.'

'Were you already intending to marry her and afraid you might put her off?'

'I wanted her to be my wife from the start.'

'Were you aware that she had many friends?'

'That's nobody's business but her own. She was free.'

'Did you talk to her about your job, your shop? You already had a shop in the Faubourg Saint-Antoine, unless I'm mistaken.'

'Naturally I talked to her about it.'

'Did you not have the idea at the back of your head that it might tempt her? By marrying you she would become the wife of a shopkeeper.'

Meurant was blushing.

'Do you realize now that it was you who wanted to get her and that you were prepared to cheat a little with that in view? Were you in debt?'

'No.'

'Any savings?'

'No.'

'Didn't she say anything to you about her wish to own a restaurant one day?'

'Several times.'

'What did you reply to that?'

'That it was a possibility.'

'Did you have any intention of giving up your job?'

'Not at that time.'

'You only decided to later, after two years of marriage, when she took up the cudgels again and mentioned an exceptional opportunity for it.'

He was distressed and Maigret went on, implacably:

'You were jealous. It was your jealousy which forced her to stay at home instead of going out to work as she wanted to. You were living in a small two-room flat then, in the Rue de Turenne. Every evening you insisted that she account for her movements during the day. Were you really convinced that she loved you?'

'I thought so.'

'Without any misgivings?'

'They didn't exist.'

'You saw quite a lot of your brother, I believe?'

'He was living in Paris.'

'Did he take your wife out?'

'We sometimes went out together, the three of us.'

'They never went alone?'

'Occasionally.'

'Your brother was living in a hotel, in the Rue Bréa, near the Place des Ternes. Did your wife ever visit his room there?'

Racked, Meurant almost screamed:

'No!'

'Did she once own a pullover, the sort people wear skiing, a pullover made of thick, white wool, hand-knitted, with reindeer designs in black and brown on it? Did she ever go out in it, in winter, wearing a pair of black slacks tight around the ankle?'

Frowning, he stared intently at Maigret.

'What are you trying to get at?'

'Answer me.'

'Yes. But only seldom. I didn't like her going out in the street in trousers.'

'Have you often met women in the streets of Paris dressed like that?'

'No.'

'Read this, Meurant.'

Maigret extracted a sheet of paper from a file, the evidence of the manageress of the hotel in the Rue Bréa. She distinctly remembered having had a guest called Alfred Meurant, who took a room in her place by the month for quite a long time, and sometimes came back for a few days since. He brought lots of women to his room. Without hesitation she recognized the photograph which was shown her, the one of Ginette Meurant. She even recalled seeing her in an unusual get-up . . .

There followed the description of the pullover and the slacks.

Had Ginette Meurant been back to the Rue Bréa recently?

The proprietress's reply: Less than a year ago, when Alfred Meurant was in Paris on a brief trip.

'It's untrue!' the man protested, pushing away the paper.

'Would you like me to give you the whole file to read? There are at least thirty statements, all from hotel proprietors, including one from Saint-Cloud. Did your brother once own a sky-blue convertible?'

Meurant's face provided the answer.

'He was not the only one. At the dance-hall in the Rue Gravilliers your wife was known to have had about fifteen lovers.'

Maigret, heavy and sombre, was filling another pipe, and it was with a gloomy heart that he had given this twist to the interview.

'It's not true!' muttered the husband once more.

'She did not ask to be your wife. She did nothing to help it. She took three weeks before she made up her mind to go out with you, perhaps because she didn't want to hurt your feelings. She went with you to the hotel when you asked her, since for her that was of little importance. You flashed before her eyes a picture of a pleasant, easy existence, security, a step up into a more or less middle-class world. You half-promised her that one day you would make her dream of owning a small restaurant come true.

'Out of jealousy, you stopped her working.

'You didn't dance. You weren't very fond of the cinema.'

'We used to go once a week.'

'The rest of the time she was forced to go by herself. In the evenings, you used to read.'

'I've always been keen on educating myself.'

'And she's always been keen on something different. Are you beginning to understand?'

'I don't believe you.'

'Nevertheless, you are sure that you spoke to nobody about the Chinese vase. And on February 27 you were not wearing your blue suit. You and your wife were the only ones with keys to the flat in the Boulevard de Charonne.'

The telephone rang. Maigret lifted the receiver.

'Yes, it's me . . .'

It was Baron at the other end of the line.

'She went out about nine o'clock, four minutes to, to be precise, and she set off to the Boulevard Voltaire.'

'Wearing what?'

'A floral dress and a brown woollen coat. No hat.'

'What happened?'

'She went into a shop that sells travelling goods and bought a cheap suitcase. She came back to the flat carrying the case. It must be warm in there because she's opened the window. Now and then I see her walking to and fro and I presume she's packing her bags.'

While he listened, Maigret was watching Meurant, who suspected that they were talking about his wife, and looked worried.

'Has anything happened to her?' he even asked at that moment.

Maigret shook his head.

'The concierge has a telephone,' Baron went on, 'so I sent for a taxi, which is now parked a hundred yards down the street in case she wants to call one.'

'Very good. Keep me in touch.'

And, to Meurant:

'Just a moment . . .'

The chief-inspector went into the duty room, spoke to Janvier:

'You had better take one of the cars and go over there, to the Boulevard de Charonne, as quickly as you can. It looks as if Ginette Meutant's about to do a bunk. Perhaps she suspects that her husband has come along here? She must be pretty scared.'

'What's his reaction?'

'I'd sooner not be in his shoes.'

Maigret would sooner have had nothing to do with the whole business.

'You're wanted on the telephone, chief-inspector.'

'Put it through here.'

It was the public prosecutor, whose conscience was also troubling him a little.

'Has anything happened?'

'They went home. Apparently they slept in separate rooms. Meurant went out early and at the moment he's in my office.'

'What have you told him? I presume he can't hear what you're saying?'

'I'm in the duty room. He's not yet sure whether to believe me. He's struggling. He's beginning to realize that he had better face reality.'

'You're not afraid he'll . . .'

'It's more than likely that he won't find her home when he gets back. She's packing her bags now.'

'And what if he does find her?'

'After the dose I've been forced to inflict on him, it's not so much her he's going to have a grudge against.'

'He's not the suicidal type?'

'Not so long as he hasn't got to the bottom of it all.'

'Are you planning to reveal it to him?'

Maigret said nothing, shrugged his shoulders.

'As soon as you have any news . . .'

'I'll telephone you or come round to your office, sir.'

'Have you read the papers?'

'Only the headlines.'

Maigret hung up. Janvier had already left. It would be wise to hold on to Meurant for a while, to prevent him catching his wife in the midst of her preparations for departure.

If he found her later on, it would be less serious. The most dangerous moment would be over. This explained why Maigret, pipe in mouth, paced up and down, strolled into the long corridor, which was not so overheated, for a while.

Then, glancing at his watch, he went into his office and found Meurant calmer, looking thoughtful.

'There is one possibility which you haven't mentioned,' Ginette's husband objected. 'One person, at least, must have known the secret of the Chinese vase.'

'The child's mother?'

'Yes: Juliette Perrin. She often visited Léontine Faverges and Cécile. Even if the old lady had said nothing to her about her money, the child might have seen . . .'

'Do you imagine that I've not thought of this?'

'Then why have you made no investigations there? Juliette Perrin works in a nightclub. She hangs around with all sorts of people . . .'

He was clinging to this hope desperately and Maigret felt unhappy about disillusioning him. Nevertheless it was necessary.

'We've made enquiries about all her contacts, without result.

'Besides there is something which neither Juliette Perrin, nor her casual or regular lovers could have procured without the very definite complicity of someone else.'

'What?'

'The blue suit. You know the child's mother?'

'No.'

'You never met her at the Rue Manuel?'

'No. I knew that Cécile's mother was a nightclub hostess, but I never had the chance to see her with my own eyes.'

'Don't forget either that her daughter was killed.'

For Meurant yet another way out had been closed. He was still looking for a solution, feeling around, determined not to admit the truth.

'My wife might have mentioned it without thinking.'

'To whom?'

'I can't think.'

'And given away the key to your flat, still without thinking, before she went to the cinema?'

Telephone. Janvier this time, a little out of breath.

'I'm phoning from the concierge's, chief. The person concerned left in a taxi with the suitcase and a rather full brown handbag. I took the cab number in any case. It's from a Levallois company and it will be easy to find it again. Baron's following her in another taxi. Shall I wait here?'

'Yes.'

'Is he still with you?'

'Yes.'

'I suppose I'd better stay put when he arrives.'

'It would be wise.'

'I'll park the car near one of the gates of the cemetery. It will be less noticed there. Are you reckoning on letting him go soon?'

'Yes.'

Meurant was still trying to puzzle it out and the effort required made the blood rush to his head. He was almost dropping with tiredness, with despair as well, but he succeeded in keeping going, and even almost in smiling.

'That my wife they're keeping their eye on?'

Maigret nodded his head.

'I suppose they'll be keeping the same sort of eye on me?'

A vague gesture from the chief-inspector.

'I haven't got a gun, I promise you!'

'I know.'

'I'm not intending to kill anyone, not even myself.'

'I know that, too.'

'Not now, at any rate.'

He got to his feet, hesitating, and Maigret realized that he was reaching the point of crisis, that the man was keeping a hold on himself so that he wouldn't burst into tears, sob, bang the walls with his clenched fists.

'Cheer up, son.'

Meurant turned his head away, walked towards the door, trying to keep his balance. The chief-inspector placed a hand on his shoulder for a second, gently.

'Come and see me when you want to.'

Meurant left the room at last without showing his face, without saying thank you, and the door shut behind him.

Baron was waiting on the quayside, ready to start shadowing him again.

Chapter Six

At midday, when he was getting ready to go home for lunch, Maigret heard his first news of Ginette Meurant.

It came through Dupeu, who telephoned from a bar in the Rue Delambre, in the Montparnasse area, near the Rue de la Gaité. Dupeu was an excellent detective, who had only one fault: he recited his reports in a monotonous voice, as if he would never come to an end, amassing so many details that you eventually listened to him with only half an ear.

'Get on! . . . Get on with it! . . .' was what you always wanted to say to him.

If you unfortunately went so far as to do so, he would appear so miserable that you immediately regretted it.

'I'm in a bar called the Pickwick, chief, a hundred yards from the Boulevard Montparnasse, and about ten minutes ago she arrived at the Hôtel de Concarneau opposite. It's a decent enough hotel which prides itself on having hot and cold running water, a bathroom on each floor. She has room 32 and she doesn't seem likely to leave in a hurry since she argued about the prices and has taken her room on a weekly basis. Unless that's all a blind.'

'She knows she's been followed?'

'I'm positive she does. In the taxi she looked round several times. As soon as they left the Boulevard de Charonne, she showed the driver a visiting-card she took out of her handbag. When we reached the Boulevard Saint-Michel, one behind the other, she leant forward to the driver. I could see her clearly through the window at the back. He immediately swung right, into the Faubourg Saint-Germain, then drove around, for nigh on ten minutes, in the little streets of Saint-Germain-des-Prés.

'I suppose she was hoping to throw me off. When she realized that wasn't possible, she gave further directions and before long her taxi drew up outside a building in the Rue Monsieur-le-Prince.'

Maigret was listening patiently, without interrupting.

'She told the cab to wait and went in. I went in a little after her and questioned the concierge. The person Ginette Meurant went to see is none other than Maître Lamblin, who lives on the first floor. She stayed in the house about twenty minutes. When she emerged, she didn't look very reassured and she immediately told the driver to bring her here. I suppose I'm to go on keeping a look-out?'

'Until someone comes to relieve you.'

Now Janvier was probably still at the Boulevard de Charonne, keeping an eye on the husband, together with Baron.

Had Ginette Meurant called on the lawyer merely to ask for his advice? Maigret suspected otherwise. Before leaving Headquarters, he gave Lucas some instructions, then made his way towards the bus station.

Seven months before, on February 27, the Meurants had hardly any money, since they were in no position to meet the bill of exchange which would fall due the next day. Apart from this, they had unpaid accounts with the neighbouring tradesmen, but that, it was true, was not unusual for them.

A few days later, when the examining magistrate had asked Meurant to name a lawyer, the frame-maker had objected that he did not have the means to pay for one and Pierre Duché had been appointed by the court.

What had Ginette Meurant been living on in the meantime? As far as the police knew – and they had watched her incoming

mail – she had received no money orders. Nor had she apparently cashed any cheques. Although she had incurred very few
expenses, had led a retired existence in her flat, she had still
had to eat, and, before the trial, she had bought the skirt and
black coat which she wore at the Assizes.

Perhaps the answer was that she had been putting money
aside herself, without her husband knowing, cheating him of
some of the housekeeping money, as quite a few wives do?

Lamblin, at the Palais, had fastened upon her. The lawyer
was smart enough to recognize that the case would have spec-
tacular repercussions, and to know that it would bring him a
great deal of publicity if he then represented the young woman.

Maigret might have been making a mistake; but he was convinced that Ginette Meurant had gone to the Rue Monsieur-
le-Prince to get hold of some money, rather than to ask for
advice.

Lamblin's reputation being what it was, he must have given
her some money, but only in dribs and drabs. He had probably
also advised her not to leave Paris but to stay calmly where
she was and wait for new developments.

The Montparnasse neighbourhood had not been chosen by
chance. Neither Meurant nor Ginette had lived round there or
were known there, and it was most unlikely that Meurant
would look for his wife in that area.

The chief-inspector returned to the peaceful atmosphere of
his flat, had lunch alone with Madame Maigret, and when he
arrived back at the Quai, at two o'clock, he had a telephone
call from Janvier to say that Meurant had not left the flat,
where everything was quiet.

He had to go to a meeting with the commissioner to discuss
a disagreeable case which had political implications, and it
was four o'clock before Janvier called again.

'Things are on the move, chief. I can't say what's going to
happen, but there will be a development soon, I'm sure. He left

home at two forty-five, carrying a number of large parcels. Although they seemed heavy, he didn't call a taxi. Still, he hadn't far to go. A little later he went into a secondhand shop, on the Boulevard de Ménilmontant, and stayed there some time talking to the owner.'

'Did he see you?'

'Probably. It was hard to keep out of sight, since the neighbourhood was pretty deserted. He sold his watch, the gramophone, some records, a pile of books. Then he went back home, came out again, this time with an enormous bundle wrapped up in a sheet.

'He returned to the same shop, where he sold some clothes, linen, blankets and some brass candlesticks.

'He's at home now. I don't think it'll be for long.'

In fact Janvier rang back in fifty minutes' time.

'He left the house once again and went to the Faubourg Saint-Antoine, to another frame-maker's. They had quite a long conversation, then the man took Meurant in his van to the Rue de la Roquette where they stopped opposite the shop you know.

'They inspected the frames one by one. The man from the Faubourg Saint-Antoine loaded a number of them into his van and handed over some bank notes to Meurant.

'I forgot to tell you that he's shaved now. I don't know what he's up to in his studio, but the car's only a few yards away, just in case . . .'

At six o'clock Maigret received his last telephone call from Janvier, who was calling from the Gare de Lyon.

'He's due to leave in twelve minutes, chief. He took a second-class ticket for Toulon. He's only got one small bag with him. At the moment he's drinking a brandy in the bar; I can see him through the window of the phone box.'

'Is he watching you?'

'Yes.'

'How does he seem?'

'Like a man who's got no time for anything else but one idea he's got fixed in his mind.'

'Make sure he really gets on that train and come back here.'

The train only stopped at Dijon, Lyons, Avignon and Marseilles. Maigret put through trunk calls to the police officers at each of the stations, gave them the frame-maker's description, specified the number of the carriage he was in. Then he called the flying squad at Toulon.

The chief-inspector in charge there was called Blanc and he was about the same age as Maigret. They knew each other well, because, before entering the Sûreté, Blanc had been at the Quai des Orfèvres.

'Maigret here. Look, old man, I hope you're not too busy. I'm arranging for the public prosecutor's department to send you a judicial warrant tomorrow, but I thought I'd better put you in the picture as soon as possible. What time does the six-seventeen from Paris arrive at Toulon?'

'Eight-thirty-two.'

'Good. In carriage number 10, that's presuming that he hasn't changed his seat during the journey, you will find a man by the name of Meurant.'

'I've been reading the papers.'

'I'd like him to be shadowed as soon as he steps off the train.'

'That's easy. Does he know the town?'

'I don't think he's ever been to the south before, but I may be mistaken. Meurant has a brother called Alfred.'

'I know the one. I've had quite a bit of trouble with him.'

'Is he at Toulon at the moment?'

'I can let you know in an hour or two. Shall I ring you back?'

'Yes, please, at my home.'

He gave his number at the Boulevard Richard-Lenoir.

'What do you know about Alfred Meurant's activities lately?'

'He normally lives at a boarding-house called "Les Eucalyptus", outside the town, quite a way out, on the hill between the Faron and La Vallette.'

'What sort of place is it?'

'The sort we keep an eye on. There are quite a few like it along the coast between Marseilles and Menton. The proprietor is a man named Lisca, known as Freddo, who was for a long time a barman in Montmartre, in the Rue de Douai. Freddo married a pretty kid, a former striptease dancer, and they bought "Les Eucalyptus".'

'Freddo does the cooking and they say he's marvellous at it, too. The house is off the main road, at the end of a lane that leads nowhere. In summer they eat outside under the trees.

'Quite respectable people from Toulon, doctors, civil servants, magistrates, go there for a meal from time to time.

'But the bulk of the customers are the crooks who live along the Coast and periodically go up to Paris.

'A few tarts too, who come down for a rest cure.

'Get the setting?'

'I get it.'

'Two frequent customers, almost all-year-round boarders, are Falconi and Scapucci.'

Two men with a string of convictions behind them, who cropped up periodically around Pigalle.

'They are great friends of Alfred Meurant's. The three of them go around openly, putting gambling machines in local bars. They also provide them with none-too-virtuous barmaids, whom they collect from all over the place.

'They have several cars at their disposal and change them pretty frequently. For some time now I've been suspecting them of selling cars in Italy which have been stolen and repainted in Paris and the suburbs.

'I've got no proof yet. My men are on to it.'

'I've good reason to think that Gaston Meurant will try and contact his brother.'

'If he asks at the right places, he won't have much trouble finding him, unless his brother's covering his tracks.'

'If my Meurant should buy a gun or try to get hold of one, I should like to be informed immediately.'

'Right, Maigret. We'll do our best. What's the weather like up there?'

'Grey and cold.'

'Sun's shining nicely here. By the way, I was almost forgetting someone. Among Freddo's customers at the moment is a fellow called Kubik.'

Twelve years before, Maigret had arrested him after a jewel robbery in the Boulevard Saint-Martin.

'It's more than likely he's involved in the jewel-theft last month on the Cours Albert-Premier in Nice.'

Maigret was also familiar with the underworld down there, and he envied Blanc a little. Like most of his colleagues, he preferred to deal with professionals, since one knew at once with them the kind of ground on which the match would be played and there were definite rules to the game.

How was Gaston Meurant, alone in a corner of his compartment, going to cope with people like that?

Maigret spent some time with Lucas, whom he put in charge of organizing the watch being kept in the Rue Delambre, and appointing detectives to go there in relays.

Ginette Meurant had spent the afternoon in her hotel bedroom, more than likely asleep. As the notice stated on the outside of the building, there was a telephone in each room, but all calls had to go through the switchboard.

According to the proprietor, who came from the Auvergne, she had not used the telephone, and he was positive that nobody at the hotel had put a call through to the South.

Nonetheless there was a special operator tapping the line at the listening-post.

Ginette had stuck it out for a long time. Either she had been extraordinarily cunning, since the murder in the Rue Manuel, or she had not once tried to communicate with the man who had been accompanying her to the Rue Victor-Massé for several months, up to and including February 26.

It was almost as if this man, suddenly from one day to the next, had ceased to exist. Nor did he, for his part, seem to have made any attempt to get in touch with her.

The police had envisaged the possibility of pre-arranged signals. They had kept a close watch on the windows in the Boulevard de Charonne, studied the position of the curtains, which might have carried some significance, the lights in the flat, the movements of people on the opposite pavement.

Nor had the man put in any appearance at the Assizes or in the neighbourhood of the Palais de Justice.

It was so remarkable that Maigret was very impressed by all this.

Now, she was going out at last, looking for a cheap restaurant in this district new to her, eating alone at a table, reading a magazine. Then she was off to buy some more at the corner of the Boulevard Montparnasse, plus a few romantic novels, climbed back up to her room where the light remained on until past midnight.

Gaston Meurant was still in the moving train. At Dijon, then at Lyons, a detective walked along the corridors, ascertained that he was still in his corner, and the information was telephoned to the Boulevard Richard-Lenoir, where Maigret stretched his arm out in the dark to pick up the receiver.

Another day was beginning. Past Montélimar, Meurant was discovering the climate of Provence, and probably his nose was soon pressed against the window, as he watched a strange landscape pass by in the sunshine.

Marseilles ... Maigret was shaving when he had the call from the Gare Saint-Charles.

Meurant was still on the train, which was now on its way again. He had not tricked them. He really was going to Toulon.

At Paris the weather remained grey, and, in the bus, people's faces were downcast or sullen. On his desk, a pile of administrative mail awaited him.

A detective – Maigret had lost track of who it was – telephoned from the bar in the Rue Delambre.

'She's asleep. The curtains are closed at any rate, and she hasn't ordered any breakfast.'

The train arrived at Toulon. Gaston Meurant, his bag in his hand, a policeman on his heels, wandered around the main square, disorientated, and eventually walked into the Hôtel des Voyageurs, where he chose their cheapest room.

A little later, they were convinced that he did not know the town, when he began to lose himself in the streets, after some trouble reached the Boulevard de Strasbourg, where he went into a large café. He ordered coffee this time, not brandy, asked several questions of the waiter, who did not seem able to furnish the required information.

At noon he had not found what he was after and, funnily enough, it was Chief-Inspector Blanc who was getting impatient.

'I wanted to have a glimpse of your fellow myself,' he said to Maigret on the telephone. 'I found him in a bar on the Quai Cronstadt. He could not have slept much in the train. He looked like some poor bloke absolutely knocked out by lack of sleep, but still obsessed by some crazy idea. He's not setting about it the right way. Up till now he's been in about fifteen cafés and bars. Each time he orders mineral water. He looks so much like a man scrounging for something that they look at him askance. He always asks the same question:

'"Do you know Alfred Meurant?"

'Barmen and waiters are immediately suspicious, specially the ones who do know him. Some just make a vague gesture in reply. Others ask:

' "What's he do?"

' "I don't know. He lives at Toulon."

'My detective who's trailing him is beginning to feel sorry for him and almost wants to tip him off.

'At the rate Meurant's going, this may last for ages and he'll make himself sick on mineral water.'

Maigret was familiar enough with Toulon to know of at least three places where Meurant would have found some news of his brother. The frame-maker was now, however, reaching the right end of the town at last. If he went farther on into the back-streets which flank the Quai Cronstadt, or again if chance took him on to Le Mourillon, he would doubtless eventually pick up the information he was hunting for so stubbornly.

In the Rue Delambre, Ginette Meurant had opened her curtains, ordered coffee and croissants and had gone back to bed to read.

She telephoned neither Maître Lamblin nor anyone else. Nor did she make any attempt to find out what was happening to her husband, or if the police were still on her own tracks.

Wouldn't she collapse under the strain sooner or later?

As for the lawyer, he took no steps, but went on with his usual activities.

Maigret had an idea, went into the duty room and walked up to Lucas.

'What time did she go and see her lawyer yesterday?'

'About eleven o'clock, if I remember rightly. I can look up my report.'

'No need. In any case, she still had time to put an advertisement in the evening papers. Get hold of all yesterday's papers, this morning's as well, and later on the evening editions. Go through the private ads.'

Lamblin did not have the reputation of being a very scrupulous man. If Ginette Meurant asked him to insert an advertisement, would he hesitate? It was unlikely.

If Maigret's hunch was a good one, it would mean that she did not know the present address of her former lover.

On the other hand, if she knew it, and if he had not moved since March, wouldn't Lamblin have telephoned him for her? Might she not have done it herself, during the twenty minutes she spent in the lawyer's office?

One detail had struck the chief-inspector ever since the spring, when the case had begun. The liaison between the young woman and the man described by Nicolas Cajou had lasted for many months. Throughout the winter they had met several times a week, which seemed to indicate that her lover lived in Paris.

Yet, nonetheless, they always met in a small hotel.

Didn't it seem likely that, for one reason or another, the man was unable to receive his mistress at his home?

Was he married? Perhaps he did not live alone?

Maigret had not found the right answer.

'It's a long shot,' he said to Lucas, 'but try to find out if a telephone call was made to Toulon yesterday from Lamblin's building.'

There was nothing else for him to do now but wait. At Toulon, Gaston Meurant was still searching and it was not until half past four, in a little café outside which men were playing bowls, that he at last got the information he was after.

The waiter pointed out the hill to him, launched into complicated directions.

Maigret already knew, by that time, that the brother, Alfred, was indeed at Toulon and had not left 'Les Eucalyptus' for over a week.

He gave Chief-Inspector Blanc his instructions.

'Have you got amongst your detectives some lad who wouldn't be recognized by those people?'

'My men never remain unknown for long, but I've one who only arrived three days ago. He comes from Brest, since his main job is to look after the naval docks. They've certainly not cottoned on to him yet.'

'Send him out to "Les Eucalyptus".'

'Right. He'll be there before Meurant; the poor chap is either trying to save money or he's got no idea of the distance, because he's set out on foot. As he'll probably get lost two or three times on those lanes up the hill . . .'

It was agony for Maigret not to be on the spot. In spite of frequent and precise reports, they only provided secondhand information.

Two or three times, during the day, he was tempted to go along to the Rue Delambre and renew contact with Ginette Meurant. He had the feeling, for no special reason, that he was beginning to get to know her better. Perhaps, now, he would find the right questions which she might finally answer?

It was still too early. If Meurant had gone off to Toulon like that without hesitating, he must have had his reasons.

During the investigation, the police had got nothing out of the brother, but that did not mean that there was nothing to be got from him.

Gaston Meurant was unarmed; this was already an established fact, and for the rest they would have to wait.

He went home, grumpy. Madame Maigret was careful not to question him, and he had dinner, in his slippers, plunged in the papers, then switched on the wireless, hunted for a less talkative station, and when he failed to find one, turned it off with a comfortable sigh.

At ten o'clock at night, they rang through from Toulon. It wasn't Blanc, who was attending a banquet, but the young detective from Brest, called Le Goënec, whom the chief-inspector of the flying squad had sent out to 'Les Eucalyptus'.

'I'm telephoning from the station.'

'Where is Gaston Meurant?'

'In the waiting-room. He's taking the night train in an hour and a half. He's paid for his hotel room.'

'Did he go to "Les Eucalyptus"?'

'Yes.'

'He saw his brother?'

'Yes. When he arrived, at about six o'clock, three men were playing cards with the proprietor's wife in the bar. There were Kubik, Falconi and Alfred Meurant, all three of them rather merry. I had arrived before him and asked if I could dine and sleep the night. The proprietor had come out of the kitchen to inspect me and finally said I could. I was wearing a haversack and told them I was hitchhiking through the Riviera looking for work.'

'Did they believe you?'

'I don't know. While waiting till it was dinner-time, I sat down in a corner, ordered some white wine and started reading. They looked across at me from time to time, but they didn't seem to worry about me much. Gaston Meurant arrived a quarter of an hour after me. It was already dark. I saw the glass door open from the garden and he remained standing on the threshold looking around him like an owl.'

'How did his brother take it?'

'He stared hard at the newcomer, stood up, threw his cards on the table, and went over to him.

'"What do you think you're doing here, boy? Who tipped you off I was here?"

'The others pretended not to be listening.

'"I must speak to you, Alfred," said Gaston Meurant.

'He added quickly:

'"Don't be afraid. I'm not after you."

' "Come on!" ordered his brother and went off towards the staircase leading to the bedrooms.

'I couldn't follow them straight away. The others had stopped talking and seemed worried; they began to look at me differently. They were probably starting to link my arrival with Meurant's.

'At all events I went on drinking my wine and reading.

'The little house, although recently repainted, is quite old, badly built, and every sound is audible.

'The two brothers shut themselves in a bedroom on the first floor and Alfred Meurant's voice was harsh and loud at first. You couldn't make out the words, but it was obvious he was very angry.

'Then the other, the one from Paris, began to speak, in a much softer voice. This lasted some time, almost without interruption, as if he was telling some prepared story.

'After winking at the men, the landlady came and set my table, as if she was trying to create a diversion. Then the others ordered apéritifs. Kubik went out to look for Freddo in the kitchen and I didn't see him again.

'I imagine that, with an eye to the main chance, he cleared out, because I heard a car engine starting up.'

'You've no idea what went on upstairs?'

'Only that they remained shut up there for an hour and a half. In the end, it seemed that it was Gaston Meurant, the one from Paris, who had the upper hand, while his brother spoke in a low voice.

'I had finished eating when they came downstairs. Alfred Meurant looked rather black, as if things hadn't worked out the way he planned, while the other fellow, on the contrary, seemed more relaxed than he had when he arrived.

' "You'll have a drink then?" Alfred proposed.

' "No. Thanks all the same."

' "You're going straight back?"

' "Yes."

'Then they both looked across at me, frowning.

' "I'll drive you down town in the car."

' "No, don't bother."

' "Do you want me to ring for a taxi?"

' "No, thanks."

'They were both talking in undertones and it was obvious that they only spoke to fill in an awkward gap.

'Gaston Meurant went out. His brother shut the door, was about to say something to the proprietress and Falconi when he caught sight of me and changed his mind.

'I wasn't sure what I should do then. I didn't dare telephone the chief and ask for further instructions. I thought the best thing to do was to follow Gaston Meurant. I went outside as if I were just going to get some fresh air after dinner, leaving my haversack behind.

'I caught up with my man, who was walking steadily down the road towards the town.

'He stopped to have a bite to eat in the Boulevard de la République. Then he went to the station, and found out the times of the trains. Last of all, he went to the Hôtel des Voyageurs, picked up his bag and paid his bill.

'Since then he's been waiting. He's not reading the newspapers, doing nothing except to stare in front of him, his eyes half closed. You can't say he looks jolly, but he doesn't exactly appear displeased with himself.'

'Wait till he gets into the train and ring me back with the number of the carriage.'

'Okay. Tomorrow morning, I'll give the chief-inspector my report.'

Inspector Le Goënec was about to hang up when Maigret thought of something.

'I'd like someone to make sure that Alfred Meurant does not leave "Les Eucalyptus".'

'Do you want me to go back there? You don't think they've rustled me?'

'All I want is for one of you to keep an eye on the house. I'd like the telephone tapped, too. If they call Paris, or any long-distance number, let me know as quickly as possible.'

The routine was starting to repeat itself, but in reverse order this time: Marseilles, Avignon, Lyons, Dijon were all alerted. Gaston Meurant was allowed to travel alone, like a grown-up, but in a way he was being passed hand from hand.

He wouldn't be arriving in Paris until half past eleven the next morning.

Maigret went to bed, felt as though he had just dozed off when his wife woke him with his first cup of coffee. The sky was clean at last and there was sunshine on the rooftops opposite. The people in the street were walking with a springier step.

'Will you be home to lunch?'

'I doubt it. I'll give you a ring before noon.'

Ginette Meurant hadn't left the Rue Delambre. She was still spending the greater part of her time in bed, only went down to eat and to stock up with magazines and novelettes.

'Nothing new, Maigret?' asked the public prosecutor, anxiously.

'Nothing definite yet, but I shouldn't be surprised if there was a development very shortly.'

'What's Meurant up to?'

'He's in the train.'

'Which train?'

'The one from Toulon. He's on his way back. He's been to see his brother.'

'What went on between them?'

'They had a long conversation, a bit violent at first apparently, but then calmer. The brother is unhappy about it. Gaston

Meurant, on the other hand, appears to know where he is going at last.'

What else could Maigret have said? He had no definite information to give the public prosecutor's office. For two days he had been groping his way round in a sort of fog, but, like Gaston Meurant, he nonetheless felt that things were coming to a head.

He was tempted to go along to the station presently and meet the frame-maker himself. Wasn't it better that he should remain at the centre of operations? And if he started following Gaston Meurant through the streets, wasn't there a risk he might spoil everything?

He chose Lapointe, knowing he would be pleased, then another detective, Neveu, who had not had anything to do with the case so far. For ten years Neveu had worked on the streets of Paris and specialized in pickpockets.

Lapointe left for the station unaware that Neveu would soon be following him.

Maigret had to give him some precise instructions beforehand.

Chapter Seven

For years Gaston Meurant, with his fresh complexion, his red hair, his blue eyes, his sheeplike expression, had been a timid man, maybe, but above all a patient, determined man, who had exerted himself, in the midst of the three million denizens of Paris, to construct some small measure of happiness.

He had mastered his craft to the best of his ability, a delicate craft which required taste and precision, and one could readily conceive how, the day on which he had set up in business on his own, even though only at the end of a yard, he had felt the satisfaction of having overcome the most difficult obstacle.

Had it been his timidity, or his cautiousness, the fear of making a mistake, that had made him for a long time keep his distance from women? During the course of his interrogations, he had admitted to Maigret that, until meeting Ginette, he had managed with little, with the very minimum, with furtive contacts of which he found himself ashamed, apart from an affair he had had when he was about eighteen with a woman much older than himself, which had only lasted a few weeks.

When the day came on which, blushing, he had at last asked a woman to marry him, he was well over thirty, and as luck would have it, she was a girl who, a few months later, when he was impatiently expecting news of a forthcoming birth, admitted to him that she could not have a baby.

He had not rebelled. He had accepted it, as he accepted the fact that she was unlike the companion he had dreamt of.

When all was said and done, they were a married couple. He was no longer on his own, even if there wasn't always a light in the window when he came home in the evening, even if it was often he who had to get the dinner ready, and although, afterwards, they had nothing to say to each other.

Her dream, on the other hand, had been of a life spent in the midst of all the activity of a restaurant of which she would be the proprietress, and he had let her have her way, without any illusions, knowing perfectly well that the experiment could only come to grief.

Then, without a sign of bitterness, he had returned to his studio and his picture-frames, compelled, every so often, to go and ask his aunt for her help.

During those years of married life, as in the years which had preceded them, there had been no trace of anger, no trace of impatience.

He would go his own way with gentle determination, bowing his big red head when he had to, holding it high again the moment fate seemed to look more kindly on him.

All told, he had built up a little world of his own around his love and he was doing everything in his power to cling on to it.

Did not all this explain the hatred which had suddenly hardened his eyes when Maigret had given his evidence at the Assizes, replacing the image he had formed for himself of Ginette with another one?

Acquitted against his will, as it were, freed on account of the suspicions which would thenceforth hang over his companion, he had yet nonetheless left the Palais de Justice with her, at her side; without linking arms, they had returned to their flat on the Boulevard de Charonne.

They had not slept in their bed together, however. Twice, three times, she had gone to speak to him, perhaps doing her utmost to tempt him, but she had gone to sleep alone in the end, while he spent most of the night awake in the dining-room.

At that time, however, he was still struggling, striving not to believe it. Perhaps he might have been able to recover confidence. But would it have lasted long? Would life have been able to start all over again as before? Wouldn't he have undergone a series of painful makeshifts, before the ultimate crisis?

He had gone by himself, without shaving, to look at the front of an hotel. To lend himself courage, he had drunk three brandies. He had hesitated once more before entering the chilly hall of the Quai des Orfèvres.

Had Maigret been wrong to speak to him in that brutal way, setting up the reaction which would have been set up anyway sooner or later?

Even had he wanted to, the chief-inspector could not have acted otherwise. With Meurant acquitted, Meurant not guilty, there was somewhere, at liberty, a man who had cut the throat of Léontine Faverges and then suffocated a little girl aged four, a murderer with enough cold blood and cunning to send another man to trial in his stead, who had been on the verge of succeeding in his plan.

Maigret had struck while the iron was hot, forcing Meurant in one shock to open his eyes, to look truth in the face at last, and it had been a new man who had left his office, a man for whom nothing mattered any longer from now on but one fixed idea.

He had gone straight ahead, feeling neither hunger nor fatigue, moving from one train into another, incapable of stopping until he should reach his objective.

Did he have any inkling that the chief-inspector had established a whole network of surveillance around him, that he had been expected at every railway station he stopped at and that there was continually someone on his heels, possibly to intervene at the last moment?

He did not seem to be concerned about it, convinced that all the wiles of the police could not prevail against his will.

Telephone call came in after telephone call, report after report. Lucas had minutely examined the private advertisements in vain. The listening-post, which was waiting for any calls Ginette Meurant might eventually make, still in the room in the Rue Delambre, had nothing to report.

There had been no call from the lawyer Lamblin, to the South, nor to any local number.

At Toulon, Alfred Meurant, the brother, had not left 'Les Eucalyptus', and had telephoned to nobody either.

They faced a blank void, a void in the midst of which there was just one silent man moving as if in a dream.

At eleven-forty, Lapointe telephoned from the Gare de Lyon.

'He's just got in, chief. He's now eating some sandwiches in the buffet. He's still got his case with him. Was it you who sent Neveu to the station?'

'Yes. Why?'

'I wondered whether you wanted him to take over. Neveu's in the buffet, too, quite close to Meurant.'

'Don't worry about him. You carry on.'

A quarter of an hour later, it was Inspector Neveu's turn to give his account.

'I did it, chief. I jostled him at the exit. He didn't notice anything. He's got a gun. A big revolver, probably a Smith and Wesson, in the right-hand pocket of his jacket. It doesn't show too much, thanks to his mackintosh.'

'Has he left the station?'

'Yes. He caught a bus and I saw Lapointe get on behind him.'

'You can come back now.'

Meurant had not called at any gunsmith's. It must necessarily have been at Toulon that he had obtained the revolver, which could therefore only have been supplied to him by his brother.

What exactly occurred between the two men, upstairs in the curious family *pension* which was used as a crooks' meeting-place?

Gaston Meurant knew now that his brother, too, had had an intimate relationship with Ginette, and yet he had not gone in order to settle accounts with him on that score.

Hadn't he hoped, in visiting Toulon, to get information about the short, very dark-haired man who, several times a week, had been used to taking his wife to the Rue Victor-Massé?

Had he some reason to think that his brother would know about it? And had he eventually found what he wanted, a name, a clue, which the police, for their part, had been searching for in vain, for several months past?

It was possible. It was probable, since he had compelled his brother to hand over a gun to him.

If Alfred Meurant had talked, in any case, it couldn't have been out of brotherly affection. Had he been scared? Had Gaston threatened him? With some disclosure or other? Or with doing him in one fine day?

Maigret asked for Toulon on the line, succeeded, after some trouble, in getting Chief-Inspector Blanc on the other end.

'It's me again, old man. I'm sorry for all the trouble I'm giving you. We may need Alfred Meurant any time now. We can't be sure of finding him when the time comes, since I shouldn't be surprised if he took it into his head to go off on a trip somewhere. At present, I've nothing to pin on him. Couldn't you have him hauled in on some more or less plausible excuse and keep him for a few hours?'

'Right you are. That's not difficult. I've always got a question or two I can ask any of his crowd.'

'Thanks. See if you can find out if he had a pretty powerful revolver and whether it's still in his room.'

'Okay. Any news?'

'Not yet.'

Maigret almost added that it wouldn't be long. He had just warned his wife that he wouldn't be home to lunch, and, feeling disinclined to leave his office, he had ordered some sandwiches from the Brasserie Dauphine.

He still felt sorry not to be outside, following Gaston Meurant in person. He was smoking pipe after pipe, impatient, ceaselessly watching the telephone. The sun was shining brightly and the yellowing leaves of the trees lent an air of gaiety to the Seine quaysides.

'That you, chief? I must be quick. I'm at the Gare de l'Est. He's deposited his case at the left-luggage office and he's just bought a ticket to Chelles.'

'In Seine-et-Marne?'

'Yes. The diesel's due to leave in a few minutes. I'd better get cracking. I'm to go on following him, aren't I?'

'What do you think!'

'No special instructions?'

What was at the back of Lapointe's mind? Had he guessed the reason for Neveu's presence at the Gare de Lyon?

The chief-inspector grunted:

'Nothing particular. Do what you think best.'

He knew Chelles, over a dozen miles outside Paris, on the banks of the canal and the Marne. He remembered there was a big caustic-soda works, in front of which you could always see loaded barges, and once when he had gone through the neighbourhood on a Sunday morning, he had noticed a whole flotilla of canoes.

The temperature had altered in the past twenty-four hours, but whoever was in charge of the central heating in the offices of Police Headquarters had not regulated the boiler accordingly, so that the warmth was stifling.

Maigret was eating a sandwich, standing in front of the window, gazing vaguely at the Seine. From time to time he took a swig of beer, cast a questioning glance at the telephone.

The train, which stopped at all stations, would be bound to take half an hour at least, perhaps an hour, to reach Chelles.

It was the detective on duty in the Rue Delambre who rang first.

'Same as before, chief. She's just gone out and is having her lunch in the same restaurant, at the same table, as if she already had her set habits.'

As far as one could tell, she still had the courage not to get into touch with her lover.

Had he given her, as long ago as February, even before the double murder in the Rue Manuel, her instructions for the future? Was she afraid of him?

Of the two of them, which was it who had had the idea of the telephone call which brought about the incrimination of Gaston Meurant?

For, at the start, he had not been suspected. He had presented himself of his own accord to the police and introduced himself as the nephew of Léontine Faverges, whose death he had just read about in the paper.

They had had no grounds for searching his home.

But someone grew impatient. Someone had been in a hurry to see the investigation take a definite direction.

Three days, four days had passed before the anonymous telephone call which revealed what would be found in a wardrobe in the Boulevard de Charonne, a certain blue suit with bloodstains on it.

Lapointe still gave no signs of life. It was Toulon which rang.

'He's in my duty room. We're asking him a few minor questions and we'll keep him until you give us further notice. We'll find some pretext all right. His room's been searched thoroughly, without a gun being found in it. Even so, my men maintain that he often carried a revolver, which has led him to be convicted twice.'

'Has he had other convictions?'

'Never anything serious, apart from proceedings for procuring. He's too clever.'

'Thanks very much. Goodbye for now. I must ring off, as I'm expecting an important call any moment now.'

He went through into the next-door office where Janvier had just arrived.

'You had better keep yourself on hand ready to leave and make sure there's a car free in the yard.'

He was beginning to regret that he had not told Lapointe everything he knew. He called to mind a film about Malaya. It had shown a native who had suddenly run amok, that's to say he had been seized in a matter of seconds by a kind of sacred madness, and walking straight ahead of him, his pupils dilated, a kris in his hand, he had killed every living thing in his path.

Gaston Meurant was not a Malay nor had he run amok. Nevertheless, for more than twenty-four hours now, had he not been pursuing a fixed idea and was he not capable of disposing of anyone who might happen to stand in his way?

At last, the telephone. Maigret leapt over to it.

'Is that you, Lapointe?'

'Yes, chief.'

'At Chelles?'

'Beyond it. I don't know exactly where I am. Between the canal and the Marne, about a mile and a half from Chelles. I can't be certain, since we took a complicated route.'

'Did Meurant seem to know the way?'

'He didn't ask anybody anything. He must have been given precise directions. He stopped now and then to look at signposts and eventually he took a lane leading to the edge of the river. Where this lane joins the former towpath, which is now only a track, there's an inn, which is where I'm telephoning you from. The innkeeper's wife has warned me that in winter she doesn't serve meals or let rooms. Her husband's the ferryman. Meurant went past the front of the house without stopping.

'Two hundred yards upstream you can just see a tumbledown cottage around which geese and ducks are waddling freely.'

'Is that where Meurant has gone?'

'He hasn't gone in. He spoke to an old woman who pointed to the river.'

'Where is he at the moment?'

'Standing at the edge of the water, leaning against a tree. The old woman's over eighty. She's known as Mother Goose. The innkeeper's wife maintains she's half mad. Her name is Joséphine Millard. Her husband's been dead a long time. Ever since, she's always worn the same black dress and it's rumoured locally that she doesn't even take it off to go to bed. When she needs anything, she goes to the market on Saturday to sell a goose or a duck.'

'Has she had children?'

'That takes us back so long ago that the innkeeper's wife can't remember. As she says, it was before her time.'

'Is that all?'

'No. There's a man living with her.'

'Permanently?'

'For the past few months, yes. Before that, he used to disappear for several days at a time.'

'What does he do?'

'Nothing. He cuts wood. He reads. He fishes. He's patched up an old canoe. Just now, he's doing a spot of fishing. I've seen him, from a distance, in the boat moored to some stakes, at the bend in the Marne.'

'What sort of man is he?'

'I couldn't make out. According to the innkeeper's wife, he's dark, thick-set, with a hairy chest.'

'Short?'

'Yes.'

There was a silence. Then, hesitantly, as if embarrassed, Lapointe asked:

'Are you coming, chief?'

Lapointe was not afraid. Was he not feeling, however, that he would have to take responsibilities beyond his powers?

'By car, it would take you less than half an hour.'

'I'll be along.'

'What am I to do, while I wait?'

Maigret hesitated, eventually decided to say:

'Nothing.'

'Shall I stay in the inn?'

'Can you see Meurant from where you are?'

'Yes.'

'In that case, stay there.'

He went into the office next door, made a sign to Janvier who was waiting. Just as he was going out, he changed his mind, went across to Lucas.

'Go up to Records and see if there's anything under the name of Millard.'

'Okay, chief. Shall I telephone you somewhere?'

'No. I don't know exactly where I'm going. The far side of Chelles, somewhere on the banks of the Marne. If you have some urgent news for me, ask at the local police station for the name of an inn about a mile and a half upstream.'

Janvier took the wheel of the small black car, since Maigret had never been inclined to learn to drive.

'Anything new, chief?'

'Yes.'

The detective did not like to press him, and after a long silence the chief-inspector muttered gloomily:

'But I don't know what exactly.'

He wasn't sure that he was in such a hurry to arrive there. He would rather not admit it, not even to himself.

'Do you know the way?'

'I once went there for lunch on a Sunday with the wife and kids.'

They drove through the suburbs, past the first vacant lots, then the first fields. At Chelles they pulled up hesitantly at a crossroads.

'If it's upstream, we should turn right.'

'Let's try it.'

Just as they were leaving the town, a police car, with its siren blaring, overtook them, and Janvier looked at Maigret without speaking.

The chief-inspector did not say anything either. Much further on, he said, chewing the stem of his pipe:

'I suppose it's all over.'

For the police car had turned off towards the Marne, which they could now glimpse between the trees. To the right, there appeared an inn, built in yellow-painted brick. A woman, who seemed highly excited, was standing on the doorstep.

The police car, unable to get any further, had parked by the side of the lane. Maigret and Janvier emerged from theirs. The woman, gesticulating, was calling out something to them which they couldn't catch.

They walked towards the cottage surrounded by geese and ducks. The local police, who had reached it before them, were challenging two men who seemed to have been waiting for them. One of them was Lapointe. The other, from a distance, looked like Gaston Meurant.

There were three local policemen, including one officer. An old woman on the doorstep was looking at all these people, nodding her head, without seeming to understand exactly what was going on. Nobody, anyway, really understood, except perhaps Meurant and Lapointe.

Automatically, Maigret glanced around to look for a body, but could see none. Lapointe said to him:

'In the water . . .'

But there was nothing to be seen in the water either.

As for Gaston Meurant, he was calm, almost happy, and when the chief-inspector finally decided to look him in the face, it was as if the picture-framer were silently thanking him.

Lapointe was explaining, both for the benefit of his chief and for that of the local police:

'The man gave up fishing, and shoved his boat off from the stakes you can see over there.'

'Who is he?'

'I don't know his name. He was wearing denim trousers and a roll-necked seaman's sweater. He began to row across the river against the current.'

'Where were you?' the local police officer inquired.

'At the inn. I was watching the scene from the window. I had just been on the phone to Chief-Inspector Maigret . . .'

He gestured to his chief, and the officer, in confusion, stepped towards him.

'I beg your pardon, Chief-Inspector. I never expected to see you here, that's why I didn't recognize you. Your inspector got the innkeeper's wife to telephone us, and all she said was that a man had just been killed and had fallen in the water. I immediately alerted the flying squad . . .'

They heard the sound of a car engine on the other side of the inn.

'There they are!'

The newcomers added to the chaos and the bewilderment. They were now in the Seine-et-Marne department and Maigret had no official standing in this case.

Nevertheless everybody turned towards the chief-inspector.

'Shall we put the handcuffs on him?'

'That's up to you, lieutenant. If I were in your place, however, I shouldn't think it necessary.'

Meurant's fever had subsided. He listened vaguely to what was being said as if it was of no concern to him. Mostly he stared at the swirling waters of the Marne, downstream.

Lapointe went on with his explanation:

'While he was rowing, the man who was in the boat had his back turned to the bank. So he couldn't see Meurant, who was standing near this tree.'

'Did you know he was going to shoot?'

'I didn't know he was armed.'

Maigret's face remained impassive. Nevertheless Janvier cast him a quick glance, as if he had suddenly begun to understand.

'The bow of the boat touched the bank. The rower stood up, seized the painter, and as he turned round he found himself face to face with Meurant, who was hardly three yards away from him.

'I can't say whether they exchanged words or not. I was too far away.

'Almost immediately, Meurant drew a revolver from his pocket and stretched out his right arm.

'The other man, standing ready to disembark, must have been hit by the two bullets, shot one after the other. He let go of the painter. His hands beat the air and he fell into the water head first . . .'

Everybody was now looking at the river. The rain, during the last few days, had swollen the water, which had a yellowish colour and in certain places there were swirling eddies.

'I asked the innkeeper's wife to notify the police and I ran across to here . . .'

'Were you armed?'

'No.'

Lapointe added, perhaps unthinkingly:

'There was no danger.'

The local police could not understand. Nor could the men from the flying squad. Even had they read the newspaper reports of the trial, they were not aware of the details of the case.

'Meurant made no attempt to run away. He remained in the same spot watching the corpse disappear, then reappear again two or three times, always a little further on, until it sank altogether.

'When I reached his side, he dropped his gun. I didn't touch it.'

The revolver was embedded in the mud of the lane, beside a dead branch.

'He said nothing?'

'Two words only:

' "It's over." '

The struggle was indeed over now for Gaston Meurant. His body seemed flabbier, his face puffy with tiredness.

He did not look triumphant, felt no need to explain himself, to justify himself. It was entirely his own affair.

In his view he had done what he had to do.

Would he have ever found peace otherwise? Would he find it from now on?

The public prosecutor's men from Melun would soon be arriving on the spot. The mad woman, on her threshold, was still nodding her head, never having seen so many people around her house before.

'It's quite likely,' Maigret said to his colleagues, 'that you may make some discoveries when you go through the cottage.'

He could have remained with them, helped in the search.

'Gentlemen, I shall send you all the information you will need.'

He would not be taking Meurant back to Paris, since Meurant no longer belonged to the Quai des Orfèvres, nor to the public prosecutor's department for the Seine district.

It would be in another law-court, in Melun, where he would appear for the second time before the Assizes.

Maigret asked Lapointe and Janvier in turn.

'Are you coming, lads?'

He shook hands all round. Then, as he was turning away, he took his last look at Ginette's husband.

Suddenly conscious of his weariness, probably, the man had leaned against the tree again and watched the chief-inspector leave, a look almost of melancholy in his eyes.

Chapter Eight

Few words were exchanged during the drive back. Several times Lapointe opened his mouth, but Maigret's silence was so deep, so deliberate, that he did not dare say anything.

Janvier was driving and, little by little, he had the feeling that things were slipping into place.

But for the difference of a mile or two, they would have been taking Gaston Meurant back themselves.

'Perhaps it's just as well that way,' murmured Janvier as if he were speaking to himself.

Maigret did not approve nor disapprove. To what, besides, had Janvier been alluding exactly?

The three of them climbed the staircase together at Headquarters, separated in the corridor, Lapointe and Janvier going into the duty room, while Maigret entered his office, where he hung his coat and hat in the cupboard.

He did not touch the bottle of brandy which he kept handy for some of his visitors. He had hardly had time to fill a pipe when Lucas knocked on the door and put in front of him a thick file.

'I found that upstairs, chief. You might say it all hangs together.'

And it did, in fact, all hang together. It was the file of a certain Pierre Millard, called Pierrot, thirty-two years old, born in Paris in the Goutte-d'Or district.

He had had his police record since he was eighteen years old, when he appeared for the first time at the Seine police-court for procuring. Later he had two other convictions on the same count, with a period in Fresnes gaol, then a conviction for assault and battery at Marseilles, and finally five years in the prison at Fontévrault, for breaking into a factory at Bordeaux and violent assault on a night-watchman who had been discovered half dead.

He was released from prison a year and a half ago. Since then, they had lost track of him.

Maigret lifted the receiver, called Toulon.

'Is that you, Blanc? Well, old man, it's all over up here. Two bullets in the hide of a certain Pierre Millard, called Pierrot.'

'A short dark fellow?'

'Yes. They are busy searching for his body in the Marne, where he fell in head first. Does the name mean anything to you?'

'I'd have to have a word with my men about it. I seem to remember that he was prowling around here a little more than a year ago.'

'That's more than likely. He came out of Fontévrault about then and was therefore prohibited from staying here. Since you've now got his name, could you perhaps put a few definite questions to Alfred Meurant? Is he still with you?'

'Yes. Do you want me to ring you back?'

'Yes, please.'

In Paris, at any rate, Millard had been prudent. Though he probably came frequently, almost every day, he was careful not to sleep the night there. He had found a safe refuge beside the Marne, in the cottage belonging to the old woman, who was probably his grandmother.

He had not budged since the double murder in the Rue Manuel. Ginette Meurant had made no attempt to visit him. She had not sent him any message. She was probably kept in the dark about his hiding-place.

If things had happened differently, if Nicolas Cajou, in particular, had not given his evidence, Gaston Meurant would have been condemned to death, or to forced labour for the rest of his life. At the best, considering the slight doubt in his favour and his unblemished past, he might have got off with twenty years.

Whereas Millard, once the verdict had been brought, could have left his hole, gone to the provinces or abroad, where Ginette Meurant could easily have joined him.

'Hello, yes . . .'

They were calling him from Seine-et-Marne. The flying squad at Gournay informed him that they had discovered the gold pieces, the bearer-bonds, and a certain number of bank notes in an old wallet.

The whole lot had been buried, hidden in a tin, in the geese and ducks' pen.

They had not yet fished out the body, which they hoped to find, like most bodies drowned in that reach, at the Chelles weir, where the lock-keeper was quite accustomed to it.

They had made some other discoveries in the old woman's house, amongst them, in the loft, an ancient trunk containing a Second Empire wedding-dress, a suit, other dresses, some made of puce or pale blue silk, embroidered with yellowed lace. The most unexpected find was a Zouave's uniform of the beginning of the century.

Mother Goose could scarcely remember anything about her family, and the death of her grandson didn't seem to have affected her. When they had spoken of taking her to Gournay for questioning, she was only concerned about her birds, and they had had to promise to bring her back the same evening.

They would probably hardly bother about her past, or her children, of whom no trace could be found.

She would probably still live for years in her cottage by the waterside.

'Janvier!'

'Yes, chief.'

'Will you take Lapointe with you and go along to the Rue Delambre?'

'Am I to fetch her here?'

'Yes.'

'You don't think I ought to take a warrant with me?'

Maigret, as an officer of Paris Police Headquarters, was empowered to sign an order to appear and he did it on the spot.

'What if she asks any questions?'

'Say nothing.'

'Shall I handcuff her?'

'Only if it's absolutely necessary.'

Blanc rang back from Toulon.

'I've just been asking some interesting questions.'

'Did you tell him of Millard's death?'

'Of course.'

'Did he seem surprised?'

'No. He didn't even bother to put on a pretence of it.'

'Did he come clean?'

'More or less. That's up to you to judge. He was careful not to say anything that might incriminate him. He admits that he knew Millard. He met him several times, more than seven years ago, in Paris and Marseilles. Then Millard copped five years and Alfred Meurant heard nothing from him.

'When he got out of Fontévrault, Millard came back to hang around Marseilles, then Toulon. He was pretty down on his luck and was trying to get back on the game. His plan, according to Meurant, was not to do the odd job any more, but to bring off something big which would set him up once and for all.

'As soon as he'd refurbished his wardrobe, he was intending to return to Paris.

'He only stayed a few weeks on the Coast. Meurant admits

that he gave him small sums, that he introduced him to his pals and that they helped him in their turn.

'As for the matter of Ginette Meurant, her brother-in-law talks of her jokingly. He apparently said to Millard, just as he was leaving:

' "If you're ever short of a woman, there's always my little sister-in-law; she's married to an imbecile and she's pretty bored."

'He swears that was all. He gave Ginette's address and also told him that she liked going to a dance-hall in the Rue des Gravilliers.

'If you can believe him, he heard no further news of Pierre Millard, nor of Ginette either.'

This was not necessarily true, but it was plausible.

'What shall I do with him?'

'Get a statement from him and release him. But don't let him out of your sight, because we'll need him for the trial.'

If there was a trial! New investigations would begin, as soon as Lapointe and Janvier brought Ginette Meurant into Maigret's office.

Would they be able to establish with sufficient certainty her complicity with her lover?

Nicolas Cajou would go to identify Millard's body, then the chambermaid, and others as well.

Afterwards, there would be the preliminary examination, then, eventually, the file would be referred to the Grand Jury.

During all that time it was more than probable that Ginette would remain in prison.

Then, one day, she would appear at the Assizes in her turn.

Maigret would be summoned as a witness once more. The jury would try to understand something of this story which was taking place in a world so different from their own familiar universe.

Before that, since the case was more straightforward and the list was not so full at the Seine-et-Marne Assizes, Maigret would be summoned to Melun.

With other witnesses he would be shut up in a gloomy, hushed room like a vestry where he would await his turn, watching the door and listening to the dull echoes from the courtroom.

He would see Gaston Meurant again between two policemen, would swear to tell the truth, the whole truth, nothing but the truth.

Would he really tell the whole truth? Hadn't there been one particular moment, while the telephone was ringing incessantly in his office, where he kept some control on all the characters, when he had accepted a responsibility which was hard to explain away?

Might he not have been able to . . . ?

In two years he would no longer have to worry about other people's problems. He would be living with Madame Maigret far from the Quai des Orfèvres and the courts where men are judged, in an old house like a presbytery, and for hours on end he would sit in a punt moored to some stakes, watching the water flow past, fishing.

His office was full of his pipe-smoke. Next door he could hear typewriters tapping away, telephones ringing.

He gave a start when there came a light tap on the door and it opened to reveal Lapointe's young figure.

Had he really jerked back guiltily, as if somebody were coming to call him to account?

'She's here, chief. Do you want to see her straight away?'

And Lapointe waited, seeing clearly that Maigret was slowly coming to from a dream – or a nightmare.

PENGUIN CLASSICS

MAIGRET AND THE GHOST
GEORGES SIMENON

'A novelist who entered his fictional world as if he were part of it'
Peter Ackroyd

Inspector Lognon – a plain-clothes detective with a reputation for misfortune – is shot in the street with the word 'ghost' on his lips. It soon emerges that he spent the night in the nearby apartment of a beautiful young woman, who has since then vanished. While the injured man fights for his life in hospital, Chief Superintendent Maigret discovers that the hapless Inspector may finally have been on to something big. And when he encounters suave art dealer Norris Jonker and his glamorous wife Mirella, Maigret begins to wonder if their strange lifestyle is the reason for Lognon's presence on the Avenue Junot.

In *Maigret and the Ghost*, Simenon's tenacious detective is perplexed by a constant stream of conflicting evidence as he explores the underground world of art collecting.

www.penguinclassics.com

read more ⓟ

PENGUIN CLASSICS

A MAN'S HEAD
GEORGES SIMENON

'Excellent … grips from the first line' *Independent*

A rich American widow and her maid have been stabbed to death in a brutal attack. All the evidence points to Joseph, a young drifter, and he is soon arrested. But what is his motive? Or is he just a pawn in a wider conspiracy?

Inspector Maigret believes the police have the wrong man and lets him escape from prison to prove his innocence. Perhaps, with Joseph on the loose, the real murderer will surface.

A deadly game of cross and double-cross has begun …

'A giant, a genius, a glorious storyteller' *Daily Telegraph*

www.penguinclassics.com

PENGUIN CLASSICS

MY FRIEND MAIGRET
GEORGES SIMENON

'The archetypal fictional detective' *Sunday Times*

A small-time crook has been murdered on a Mediterranean island.
He was a nasty piece of work – a drunken thug, pimp and thief. Yet
just before he died he was heard boasting in a crowded bar about his
policeman 'friend' Maigret.

When Inspector Maigret hears about this, he decides to take a little
island holiday to find out what's going on. Nobody there seems to have
a motive for killing Pacaud - not the old English lady and her male
'secretary' nor the ageing prostitute and the Dutch anarchist.

But plenty of them have secrets they'd prefer to keep hidden …

www.penguinclassics.com

PENGUIN CLASSICS

THE LOST WORLD
ARTHUR CONAN DOYLE

A land before time – a journey beyond belief …

Unlucky in love, but desperate to prove himself in an adventure, journalist Ed Malone is sent to test the infamous and hot-tempered Professor Challenger on his bizarre South American expedition findings – not least his sketches of a strange plateau and the monstrous creatures that appear to live there.

But rather than being angry at his questions, Challenger invites him along on his next field trip. Malone is delighted: until it becomes clear that the Professor was telling the truth about the terrible lost world he has discovered.

Will they all survive the terrifying creatures on the island? And will anyone ever believe what they saw there?

'A classic of its kind' Arthur C. Clarke

www.penguinclassics.com

PENGUIN CLASSICS

THE MAN WHO WAS THURSDAY
G. K. CHESTERTON

Can you trust yourself when you don't know who you are?

In a park in London, secret policeman Gabriel Syme strikes up a conversation with an anarchist. Sworn to do his duty, Syme uses his new acquaintance to go undercover in Europe's Central Anarchist Council and infiltrate their deadly mission, even managing to have himself voted to the position of 'Thursday'.

When Syme discovers another undercover policeman on the Council, however, he starts to question his role in their operations. And as a desperate chase across Europe begins, his confusion grows, as well as his confidence in his ability to outwit his enemies.

But he has still to face the greatest terror that the Council has – its leader: a man named Sunday, whose true nature is worse than Syme could ever have imagined.

www.penguinclassics.com

PENGUIN CLASSICS

THE THIRTY-NINE STEPS
JOHN BUCHAN

'Go into a bookshop and pick up *The Thirty-Nine Steps* and I guarantee you will read it to the end' *Mail on Sunday*

Chased by a killer, wanted by the police, Richard Hannay is on the run …

He has been feeling bored with London life – until he discovers a dead man in his flat, skewered to the floor with a knife through his heart. Only a few days before the victim had warned him of an assassination plot that could bring the country to the brink of war. An obvious suspect for the police and an easy target for the murderer, Hannay goes on the run in his native Scotland. There, on the wild moors, he must use all his wits to stay one step ahead of the game – and warn the government of the impending danger before it is too late …

'Probably the best-known thriller in English … action-packed'
Good Book Guide

www.penguinclassics.com

PENGUIN CLASSICS

RUPERT OF HENTZAU
ANTHONY HOPE

The swashbuckling sequel to *The Prisoner of Zenda*

When honour is at stake, the fight is to the death.

Rudolf Rassendyll, having heroically saved the kingdom of Ruritania and nobly given up the hand of the beautiful Princess Flavia, has returned to his normal life in England. But when, three years later, Flavia, now the unhappily married Queen of Ruritania, sends him a love letter, it is stolen by the exiled villain Rupert Hentzau. Rudolf's former adversary has been waiting for the chance to have his revenge, and this provides the perfect opportunity to stir up trouble.

Rudolf must return to the troubled kingdom to defeat Hentzau, where he is embroiled once more in a world of deception, intrigue, deadly swordfights and torn loyalties. With the stakes higher than ever, will he pay the ultimate price?

www.penguinclassics.com

PENGUIN CLASSICS

THE CASTLE OF OTRANTO
HORACE WALPOLE

A haunted castle and a ruined bloodline …

Manfred, wicked lord of Otranto Castle, is horrified when his son is crushed to death on his wedding day. But rather than witness the end of his line, as foretold in a curse, he resolves to send his own wife to a convent and marry the intended bride himself.

However, Manfred's lustful greed will be disturbed by the terrifying omens that now haunt his castle: bleeding statues, skeletal ghouls and a giant sword – as well as the arrival of the rightful prince of Otranto.

www.penguinclassics.com

PENGUIN CLASSICS

PAUL CLIFFORD
EDWARD BULWER-LYTTON

'It was a dark and stormy night …'

Paul Clifford leads a double life. By day he is a fashionable man about town, the toast of genteel society. By night, he is 'Captain Lovett', a dashing masked highwayman, robbing unsuspecting travellers on moonlit roads with his band of fellow brigands.

When Clifford falls in love with the beautiful, auburn-haired Lucy, the daughter of a wealthy squire, he wonders if he should abandon his life of vice. But there are many obstacles in his path: his sly love-rival Lord Mauleverer, dark secrets from the past, and the threat of the hangman's noose …

www.penguinclassics.com

read more

PENGUIN CLASSICS

JACK SHEPPARD
WILLIAM HARRISON AINSWORTH

A master of drinking, whoring, theft – and escape!

While Jack Sheppard seems marked from birth for a terrible end, his wit and charm might just be able to cheat fate. Fate, however, seems eager to cheat him out of an honest living, when Jack begins visiting the notorious Black Lion, drinking den of the worst criminals in London. Soon he is one of the most famous scoundrels in the city – not for his crimes, but for the wonderful fact that not one of the King's fine prisons can hold him.

But Jack's luck will have to run out eventually…

www.penguinclassics.com

He just wanted a decent book to read ...

Not too much to ask, is it? It was in 1935 when Allen Lane, Managing Director of Bodley Head Publishers, stood on a platform at Exeter railway station looking for something good to read on his journey back to London. His choice was limited to popular magazines and poor-quality paperbacks – the same choice faced every day by the vast majority of readers, few of whom could afford hardbacks. Lane's disappointment and subsequent anger at the range of books generally available led him to found a company – and change the world.

'We believed in the existence in this country of a vast reading public for intelligent books at a low price, and staked everything on it'
Sir Allen Lane, 1902–1970, founder of Penguin Books

The quality paperback had arrived – and not just in bookshops. Lane was adamant that his Penguins should appear in chain stores and tobacconists, and should cost no more than a packet of cigarettes.

Reading habits (and cigarette prices) have changed since 1935, but Penguin still believes in publishing the best books for everybody to enjoy. We still believe that good design costs no more than bad design, and we still believe that quality books published passionately and responsibly make the world a better place.

So wherever you see the little bird – whether it's on a piece of prize-winning literary fiction or a celebrity autobiography, political tour de force or historical masterpiece, a serial-killer thriller, reference book, world classic or a piece of pure escapism – you can bet that it represents the very best that the genre has to offer.

Whatever you like to read – trust Penguin.